HOW **NOT** TO DESTROY YOUR CAREER IN MUSIC

Avoiding the Common Mistakes Most Musicians Make

BRUCE HARING

 lone eagle    THE REPORTER

HOW NOT TO DESTROY YOUR CAREER IN MUSIC
Avoiding the Common Mistakes Most Musicians Make

LONE EAGLE PUBLISHING COMPANY™
5055 Wilshire Blvd.
Los Angeles, CA 90036
Phone 323.525.2369 or 800.815.0503
www.hcdonline.com

Printed in the United States of America
10 9 8 7 6 5 4 3 2 1

Cover design by zekeDESIGN
Book design by Carla Green
Edited by Steve Atinsky

Library of Congress Cataloging-in-Publication Data
Haring, Bruce
How not to destroy your career in music : avoiding the common mistakes most musicians make / by Bruce Haring.
    p. cm.
  ISBN 1-58065-064-3
  1. Music—Vocational guidance. 2. Music trade. I. Title.

  ML3795.H3 2005
  780'.23'73—dc22   2005045180

Books may be purchased in bulk at special discounts for promotional or education-al purposes. Special editions can be created to specifications. Inquiries for sales and distribution, textbook adoption, foreign language translation, editorial, and rights and permissions inquiries should be addressed to: Steve Atinsky, Lone Eagle Publishing, 5055 Wilshire Blvd., Los Angeles, CA 90036 or send e-mail to info@loneeagle.com.

Lone Eagle Publishing Company™ is a registered trademark.

From the Publishers of ▼**vnu** business media

To my wife, Debbie.
Couldn't DIY without you.

CONTENTS

FOREWORD

I love the title of this book, *How Not to Destroy Career in Music.*

Making a living doing nothing but music isn't so hard. The only two ways to "ruin" your music career are to never learn, or give up. But if you're willing to learn, and you never give up, you'll do just fine. It's not that hard. You'd be surprised, but just by using a little common sense and people skills, you'll already be ahead of 90 percent of the musicians out there.

Rebel against the slacker cliché. Do what you say you'll do, follow-up on every contact, completely pursue every opportunity, practice more than is necessary, never stop learning, and take an honest interest in all the people around you.

Not the organized or social type? It's worth it for you to learn. (If you can learn music, you can learn anything!)

Doing these things will guarantee you a great, long career in music.

— Derek Sivers, founder,
CD Baby and HostBaby

1
THE CHANGING OF THE GUARD

You've read the stories and heard the reports:

The Music Industry Is Dying!

No Artist or Songwriter Will Be Able to Make a Living Because Music Is Too Easy to Get for Free!

Record Companies Are Going Out of Business and Retail Stores Are Closing!

Radio Consolidation Has Choked Off Access for All But the Largest Players!

THE CONCERT INDUSTRY HAS PRICED TICKETS OUT OF THE REACH OF MOST CONSUMERS!

Blah, blah, blah.

The stories are only partially correct. Yes, the music industry is changing. Most big record labels owned by multinational corporations are dying under the crushing weight of high overhead and declining sales.

Yes, it's true that many concert promoters and venues are losing money because no one can afford their high-priced tickets.

And it's also correct that a vast number of record retailers are hurting because fewer people are buying expensive CDs, preferring to steal music from the online networks that allow you to swap without compensation to the creators or copyright holders of the compositions.

But new opportunities are emerging as a result of these changes. The opportunities won't be available to those entrenched in the old system. Only those able to be lean, mean, and fast will be able to seize the moment.

Music isn't dying. Rest assured, as long as the young men and women of the tribe continue to gather to drink the wacky juice and dance to someone beating on a log, music will survive. And as a result of the young men and women gathering in that fashion, many people will still make a living from performing, promoting, producing, and distributing music. Innovative companies and new methods of delivery will emerge to transmit new sounds and old favorites.

The big difference between those who will thrive in the coming years and the large entities that are currently suffering from the change in the way business is done is simple:

It's all about organization.

The moneymakers of tomorrow will be extremely smart about business structures and will keep a tight control over the amount of money they spend versus the amount of money they take in. Risk versus reward will be carefully measured and expenses will be prudent and justified.

The companies that will not survive will continue to pay bloated executive salaries and sign more acts than they can work effectively, wasting huge amounts of money on signing bonuses for acts that will never equal the expenditures outlayed with records sold.

The companies that will not survive will rely on expensive commercial radio and retail promotions, both designed to cram music down consumer throats.

The companies that will not survive will insist on getting their artists to sign contracts that retain rights to the master recordings until the end of time. They will view things with a short-term eye on quarterly profits, for that is what their public shareholders demand. In short, the money losers of the future will continue to do business in the way that most large record labels have done for decades. And the vast majority of people aligned with that system will experience disappointment, defeat and discouragement as a result of such stubborn resistance to the winds of change.

Of course, by the very act of picking up this book, we suspect that you will not be among those who will be cursing their fate in this brave new world of selling music.

The goal of this book isn't to illustrate every step a musician needs to take to achieve success. And it's not meant as the ultimate how-to guide on what she or he needs to avoid in order to have a career in music. Although we will cover a lot of that information, there are many fine books on the market that detail the various processes and legalisms of the complex, multinational and multi-billion dollar recorded music industry.

No, instead of a formal how-to, most of this book is designed to be a *what if*.

What if everything you knew or thought you knew about starting or sustaining a career in the music industry had changed?

What if the old way of creating and sustaining a music act was no longer the best way to sustain a rich and long-lasting career in the business?

Because of very recent changes in the music industry, it's crucial that readers understand that building a career has changed radically from what it was even five years ago.

It is now time to re-examine the traditional notions of what goes into creating, growing and sustaining a long-term career in the record industry, in order to avoid the pitfalls created by the abrupt changes in the marketplace.

Realizing that the international music industry is a business in transition is the first step toward adapting to its new realities.

It is perhaps the hardest step of all to take, because of the sheer number of people who deny that any change is happening.

There are many who cling to the old ways of doing things and sustain a belief in the myths that surround the recording business, hoping against hope that the system will go back to the comfortable niche they have enjoyed for years.

Musicians looking for a long-term career should ignore these little men and women behind the curtain. They preach old values and embrace the way things used to be done out of self-interest. A change in the way business is done means that their power base and large salaries will vanish sooner than retirement arrives.

In order to understand the changes now taking place, you must first look at the reality, not the glamour, of the record industry. Do not be over-awed by the vast corporate machinery that has been built up over the last few decades, when the music industry turned into a multinational corporate monolith.

During those years, the standard business practice for large record companies was to have one worldwide hit generate enough revenue to cover up for numerous failures.

While the performer behind that worldwide hit may have been momentarily happy, such a system ruined more than a few artists careers by focusing on short-term success, leaving many people disillusioned.

And, more often than not, the result of that short-term success is lowest-common-denominator entertainment over true artistic achievement. Think not? Check out what's playing on commercial radio now and ask yourself whether this is the best that music can offer. And remember that while vanilla may be the most popular ice cream, it is not necessarily the best ice cream.

Today's music scene is the product of an industry that has grown too big. It has lost sight of the reason for its existence and moved away from being run by people immersed in music's creation.

Instead, it has been taken over by multinational corporations, so-called tastemakers of dubious heritage and grounding, and more than a few hustlers whose goal is financial rather than artistic.

As a result, the music industry has devolved into a weird parody of the worst excesses of the music business as imagined by Hollywood movies and cheap paperbacks. It's swarming with people whose respect and compassion for the art and its artists is largely lip service.

The only good news arising from that sad state of affairs is that the real grassroots of the business still exists. And thanks to technology, it's now easier than ever to avoid that system and build your own business in music.

But doing so takes a different mindset than most musicians have followed over the last five decades.

The changes in the music industry arrived gradually. Although many music companies became quite large in the 1950s through early 1970s, they still retained a regional flavor and employed a healthy number of people who knew their way around a recording studio.

The record labels were akin to mom-and-pop grocery stores, turning out acts with which record company owners had a strong, personal bond.

But by the mid-1980s, the record industry had evolved from a business run by creative people to one whose structure, financing, and direction were controlled by six multinational corporations: Time Warner, Bertelsmann, Matsushita, Thorn-EMI, Philips, and

Sony. Those six major distributors, which accounted for roughly 95 percent of the record business at that time, dealt in such non-music product as refrigerator rentals, electronic hardware, and book clubs.

These new companies also spawned a new breed of record executive. The street-oriented entrepreneurs who had built the music business were increasingly pushed aside in favor of bottom-lined obsessed corporate officers whose credentials were largely burnished outside of the entertainment world.

By the early 1990s, the frenzy of corporatization in the music business had reached its height. Drunk on the growth spurred by the replacement of vinyl records with compact discs, the music industry had become a $30 billion dollar worldwide empire.

It was also becoming a victim of its own success.

Because of such enormous growth and the removal of the pioneers of the business in favor of more corporate executives, the record industry began to lose a great deal of respect for the artist. Music became "product," something that was pushed to retail, radio, and other outlets with the same zeal as Cornflakes.

Naturally, the art of music suffered. Bands were signed and then discarded at a faster pace than ever, as the record companies searched for the one act out of 20 that would sell at a pace that would justify all the losers and keep the bottom line healthy.

No longer did the corporate giants who dominated the business have time to nurture artists through several albums. The economics of promoting, publicizing and marketing a band had become too great to afford that luxury.

Moreover, there weren't many executives with job stability. If they supported acts on artistic merit rather than immediate profits, they could lose their cushy job and expense account. That led to a follow-the-pack mentality in which the trend became to sponsor someone so safe, so homogenous, that you couldn't be blamed if it crashed and burned.

Despite those changes, many musicians still made "getting signed" their ultimate goal, ignoring the obvious damage to their long-term interests that being part of a large roster would cause.

Star-struck and disempowered by the increasing consolidation of the industry into big business, musicians lost sight of the fact that they controlled the business, since they were creating the product. Thus, many adopted an employee mentality, helpless to achieve success without direction from above.

The recording industry's churn-and-burn strategy of artist development worked well from an economic standpoint up until the late 1990s. Then the financial party began to slow, thanks to a number of factors.

First, CD sales began to level off. No longer were quarterly profits fueled by fans replacing their vinyl records with CDs.
But more important, the record industry was paying scant attention to the development of the commercial Internet.

The lack of savvy regarding the online world would cost the recording industry several billion dollars. The record industry was late to recognize the phenomenon of online file sharing, viewing it as a distant threat that would take years to develop and would give ample warning of its arrival.

They guessed wrong. And worse, when they did take notice and began to react, they chose to fight rather than embrace the new technology.

They adopted a terrible public relations strategy that served mostly to paint themselves as villains to the masses of teenagers and young adults who thoroughly enjoyed the practice of trading music via the Net.

By the time the record industry had begun developing viable alternatives to the wave of free file-swapping systems available online, it was too late. The practice of getting music for free had become ingrained in the culture and no amount of threats, legal actions or foot stomping could put the toothpaste back in the tube.

By 2004, battered by the most severe sales slump in its history, the record industry consolidated from a Big Six to a Big Four. Thousands of layoffs resulted at record companies and the ancillary businesses that supported them. And there was scant hope that things would turn around soon.

"The industry has to figure out how to reinvent itself," said Dennis Laventhal, the publisher of *Hits* magazine, in an interview with Reuters news service. "The traditional model is obviously broken and the labels have to figure out how the new technology and the older, established music business intersect in a profitable way."

Unfortunately, it was probably too late to change for many of those big companies.

While big companies suffered misfortune from technology's turn of events, new opportunities opened up for smaller, street-savvy, and low overhead musicians and entrepreneurs.

Since the dawn of music, most musicians have sought to finance their careers through patrons, wealthy people whose largesse was used to support the creation of art for their own enjoyment and exploitation. Through these patrons, musicians, and other artists were able to devote the necessary time toward creating new and entertaining works instead of becoming, say, a blacksmith's apprentice and playing the lute part-time.

In olden times, such funding meant that a musician could continue with live performances and songwriting. In later years, as technology transformed the world and enabled new means of music reproduction, such funding meant creating songs that could be presented on piano rolls and sheet music as well as performed live.

And, finally, in the 20th century, musicians started to seek patrons by finding a recording company that would agree to reproduce the music on pieces of material known as records.

The myth about signing such a deal with record companies quickly superceded reality. Musicians, most of them creative types whose focus extended not to the business world but to more physical and spiritual things, often ignored the ramifications of what they were doing when entering into such deals.

Blinded by the strong urge to be able to devote time to create music—and perhaps a bit star-struck by the glamour, attention and, yes, sex, drugs, and rock 'n roll that was implicitly promised as part of the deals—musicians made it their goal to get a "deal," which was widely interpreted among the tribe as the only way to succeed in music.

Little did those musicians who signed such "deals" realize that they were signing away their life's work in return for a few upfront coins, with most of that money quickly evaporated by the need to pay a growing army of middlemen whose presence was deemed essential— an attorney, a manager, a roadie, an engineer, a producer.

While some musicians received immediate gratification from such deals, basking in the glow of acceptance by an authority deemed as a gatekeeper to popular taste, in truth they were largely allowing themselves as well as their works to be unjustly exploited.

Through various legal and accounting means, the musicians under such "deals" were reduced to the status of their medieval ancestors, forced to largely rely on performances for their living while the recordings and publishing made money for the patrons.

Typically, a musician realized her or his predicament only when it was late in their career. At that point, a musician whose art had achieved some success would realize that they had created wealth and built businesses for other people, not themselves and their families.

When their ability to tour dried up, they were often left with little money generated from the time spent creating music. Which meant it was time to find a day job and move on to another career.

This is not to say that a small portion of skillful musicians did not make millions from the same system. But it's interesting to note that many of those "successful" artists still wind up auditing and suing their record companies and managers for poor accounting and mismanagement, leaving the impression that the amounts of money generated were so enormous that the artists received spillover money from the vast pot controlled by the record and publishing companies rather than their full and rightful earnings.

It's instructive to see how the modern record industry system works in the long-term from an artist's perspective.

Joyce Moore is the wife of R&B legend Sam Moore. She's been in a tireless battle for years over various forms of payment owed to her husband and other older musicians from the dawn of the rock 'n roll age.

"Sam signed a deal that was probably close to standard at the time for his artistry," said Moore, referring to her husband's 1960s deal with Memphis-based Stax Records. "So even if it was a really bad deal, I don't think it was any worse a really bad deal than anybody else signed at the time. They (the artists) didn't know not to be grateful for what they got. That, plus the fact that there was never the expectation that this was a form of music with any longevity. It was hit, grab and run. It was a cash game, with a lot of guys selling out of the trunks of their cars, and they weren't bootlegging; that's how they sold their records. They would go on the road with a supply of inventory and if they didn't break, that's what they sold."

Still, Moore contends, even by understanding the how and why of early record industry deals, "that doesn't excuse that it happened. Because the businessmen of the record industry knew what they were doing, and they knew who they were doing it to."

Even with an audit, Moore lamented, the odds were slim that a full accounting would uncover everything owed to her husband.

"I don't think there's an artist that goes into an audit that doesn't find the accounting is off at least between 25-40 percent," Moore said.

"That's kind of the industry standard. That's how it works. They don't deny it. They just demand that you find it. And if you don't go in the maze, you don't get the cookie at the end of the maze. There's more to it than that. There's their ability to frustrate an audit."

Moore cited the need for artists to challenge the record company's accounting every time they received a royalty statement. Otherwise, the count proposed is the count that is deemed ratified by the artist.

"So there are many, many artists that don't know they must do that. There are many artists who cannot afford to do an audit. There are many artists who even if they could afford it, they can't go back far enough to where it would have the impact. There's no point. So it's a very, very tough situation."

Moore, one of the greats of R&B, has had some tough times.

"Over the years, there have been a lot of times we've bitten bullets and held our breath and lost condos and things and stuff, but somehow we'd get smiled on just in the nick of time. And believe me, he's been luckier than most of his peers."

A prominent music industry attorney, who asked that he not be named because he continues to work with major record labels, agreed with Moore.

"I think that there's an institutionalized system of errors that always seem to favor the label," said the attorney. "In fact, once when the Beach Boys had left Warner Bros. Records and signed with Columbia, we had done an audit of Warners and there's all this junk in the statement that Warners refused to settle on, because they were very upset at the Beach Boys and the manner in which they left. So we brought a lawsuit that was basically a bad faith lawsuit that said that all record companies and all of Warners royalty statements are intentionally under-accounted to artists. And we asked for punitive damages. And then Warners settled the case before it went very far."

Every company has little tricks that they use, the attorney continued. "First of all, royalty accounting provisions are very complicated, so they're difficult to understand to begin with. And by the time they get passed down to a clerk, I can see how mistakes get made. But what ends up happening is it's always the same mistakes and they're always in favor of the record company. So you don't have to be a real smart detective to figure out what's going on."

There were attempts by stalwart individuals to build alternatives to the entrenched system. The punk/hardcore scene of the early '80s, the "new age" music movement, the Contemporary Christian market, the "AmerIndie" alternative music cluster of the mid 1980s and other genre-based sounds devised ways to reach their audience when the mainstream ignored them.

Many of the acts and record labels were eventually co-opted by the major record labels, who purchased success rather than created it.

But even though these circuits developed, they still suffered from many of the same problems that existed in the mainstream record industry. Bad deals abounded and few of the so-called alternatives sustained themselves as separate entities. A few became rich and most artists were reduced to making a living from things other than music.

Fortunately, a growing awareness of the inequities of record label "deals" and the dawn of the Internet have awakened a vast number of musicians. They now realize the opportunity that has come into being: the end of the monopoly record companies have on the most crucial element of music exploitation, distribution.

Now, thanks to the Internet, it is entirely possible for a musician to reach a large audience without signing away the rights to their compositions. To assist them in spreading the word, they can use the growing number of independent middlemen that have sprung up offering publicity, marketing, promotion and sales services to the content creator, the musician.

The biggest change from the days of yore is that you can control your destiny and have a long career in the business you love.

And, if they so choose, they can judiciously license their creations to larger companies on their own terms, retaining a large measure of control over their works.

In the coming pages, we'll examine this emerging world of building your own business by selling music. Yes, there's a lot of work involved, a great deal of risk, and there's just as much likelihood that you won't achieve success as there was in signing with a record company.

But the biggest change from the days of yore is that you can control your destiny and have a long career in the business you love. You will call the shots and decide when and how to license your music.

You'll be building a business that potentially can enrich your family for generations to come, an asset that puts you in control, rather than standing with your hat in your hands and poring over royalty statements.

This empire of your own does not exclude the possibility of working with a large, multinational recording company. But it will enable you to deal with them from a position of strength, negotiating terms that are more favorable to your future while not relinquishing all your rights in your creative works.

Under the plans we will present, in the worst case scenario, you can have a lot of fun and have a fair market test of your music's ability to reach a larger audience.

You may ultimately discover that your true talent in music lies not in the creative end, but by constructing a business that will help your fellow musicians achieve success while exposing the world to the most joyous gift you can give it, new music.

If you take one thing away from this book, take this idea: the key to long-lasting success in the business is control of your greatest assets, your songs and the recordings of your songs. They are the lifeblood of the music business. If you control your copyrights and judiciously license them for short terms, you will be the one who reaps the greatest benefit from your creative work, not an army of middlemen who nibble away at your margins, giving you the financial death of a thousand pecks.

The artist formerly and recently known as Prince said it best. In a discussion concerning his decision to align himself with a major record label after building his own independent recording company, Prince noted that none of the record companies he negotiated with on his second go-round dared to ask him about owning his master recordings as part of any deal with him.

"When I meet with a label now, they already know they're not going to be owning anything," he told *Rolling Stone* magazine. "Maybe at one time they could get Little Richard for a new car and a bucket of chicken. We don't roll like that no more."

In other words, the right way to rock means learning the right way to roll.

HOW NOT TO RUIN YOUR MUSIC CAREER

1. Focus on the reality of any deal, not the hype.

2. Do not sell your compositions. License for the short-term.

3. Understand that most record companies do not focus on long-term careers.

2
DEFINING SUCCESS

It takes a particular mindset to thrive in the unforgiving arena of popular opinion. But that's a big part of the business you've chosen to pursue, so a few words of advice are in order.

First, understand that the definition of success in music comes from within rather than by some financial measuring stick. There are people who are happy just performing on a regular night at their favorite local nightclub. There are musicians who find nothing but emptiness and despair on worldwide stadium tours.

For many, if not most musicians, their greatest satisfaction comes from making music that is heard and responded to by appreciative audiences. The joy comes from testing the limits of your creative abilities by striving to induce someone to applaud, to purchase your record, to enthuse and emote and gain aspirations from your work. All of that can be achieved no matter your sales level.

Consider that, even at the very top of the music industry, success requires constant examination of your values and motives.

Wayne Kramer is one of the founders of the MC5 and a successful solo artist who has sustained a long career in music.

"There's a great lie in rock and roll and the lie is that if you work real hard, if you have talent, that somehow you'll be discovered and that you'll be delivered and that all of those problems you have in your life will be met and overcome," he told a DIY Convention audience.

Kramer related how he went to a web site for the U.S. Bureau of Labor and Statistics that details various jobs in the U.S. What he discovered opened his eyes to the true nature of success.

"You know, there are about 50,000 professional musicians working in America today, so about 250,000 in all related industries," Kramer said. "The median earning is about $40,000 a year. But I noticed there was no job category for rock star because it doesn't exist. It's a lie. It's a myth that we sell mostly out of Hollywood. Do it yourself, that's what creating a career is all really about. Because everything that we do is do it yourself."

Kramer is not alone in his thinking.

Derek Sivers is the founder of CDBaby, one of the most popular online sellers of independent music. To date, CDBaby has delivered over $10 million dollars to musicians who sell via the site.

Sivers attributes success in music not to being coronated by a larger company, but to persistence. "People who actually go out there and try something. I think a lot of people feel paralyzed. They have that feeling of, 'I don't know what to do next.' A lot of people try a couple of the very typical things, like put up some fliers on telephone polls for a gig. But the artists that are most successful are the ones that go out there and do lots of stuff. It's almost like you can do no wrong as long as you're doing something to let the world know you exist. And also having the guts and confidence to try new and unique things."

Aimee Mann has sustained a long career through various peaks and valleys of public taste, most recently blazing her own path as an independent artist who controls her own work.

"Taking control of your own fate is a very daunting task," Mann says. And she admits a lot of her peers don't have the will-power to create their own business.

"People that have deals with major labels can't get out of them, even if they want to," Mann said. "But if they could get out of them, a lot of people are very wary about just really jumping into the fray and doing it themselves because they think it's going to be a lot of work. And there's this kind of feeling that you get from being on a major label where you feel like you're somehow protected. It's like, 'They know what they're doing.' And people are really reluctant to leave the warm house of the record company dad."

Ultimately, some musicians adapt to their circumstances. Some don't care, content to cruise on autopilot and hope for the best. But some, like Mann, realize that true artistic freedom comes only when you control your own artistic destiny.

"Psychologically, it was such a torment to constantly have my music critiqued or analyzed for its commercial potential without ever having it really be heard," she said. "I'm just not somebody who reacts well to being told what to do."

Kramer, Sivers and Mann are essentially saying the same thing. The reason that most people turn to outside help to sell their music is that they feel the need for reassurance that they're following the right path. It's so much easier to hand over responsibility to someone else. That way, if the ball is dropped, the finger can be pointed at someone else. Instead of where it really belongs. At yourself.

You are the prime mover for everything that happens in your career. And while good business management practices call for delegation of duties at times, the key word in your career is management. You have to closely manage every step of the process in order to make adjustments when things are not achieving the desired results.

That's why one of the most important first tasks in NOT ruining your career is finding people you can trust and work with, even in a do-it-yourself situation. Building a career takes a long time. You will ostensibly be working with your initial cohorts for some time, so you have to look at any association in the same manner you would if you were opening a car wash or 7-11.

Will your bandmates show up on time and do the hard work necessary toward building a career? Will your manager do what he says when he says it? Will your attorney look out for your best interests and avoid conflicts of interest? Hard questions to answer and you'll often have to go with your gut instincts, because results are the best measure of success and honesty.

Russell Simmons is one of the most successful entrepreneurs in Hollywood. A former party promoter in Queens, he became the manager of Run-DMC and parlayed that success into a multimedia empire that embraces film, TV, music, fashion, and more.

Why was he successful?

"It's certainly not because I'm as smart as most people," said Simmons. "Cause that ain't true. I tell kids all the time, 'All you have to do is keep doing it.' You start with an idea; that idea on the first night doesn't do shit. The second night your friends are laughing. The third night, you find some indication that it's going to be worth something, and then finally, ten years later it becomes worth something. Twelve years later, it's really successful. It's about sticking with it."

Despite such planning, sometimes bad things happen to even talented and successful artists who have paid close attention to their career.

Jonatha Brooke found that out in the middle of a national tour for her critically acclaimed record, *10 Cent Wings*. Her first single, *Secrets and Lies*, had just charted in the Triple AAA radio format and it seemed like her momentum was building.

The first leg of her tour ended and Brooke headed home for a well-deserved rest before another month of road work.

And that's when MCA Records decided to drop her contract.

An artist that has a major label record contract often feels a false sense of security. In theory, the record label brings to bear a large number of resources on the artist's behalf, including a staff that will work marketing, publicity, promotion, and retail angles to sell their album.

In reality, such services are assigned only to "priority" acts, which are the albums that the record company has chosen to focus on for that particular moment. Because every quarter's financial results are vital for publicly-traded companies, even great artists with great albums can be bypassed by the system in favor of promoting works that have a higher potential to quickly sell millions of records, rather than thousands or even hundreds of thousands.

Such was the case with Brooke, an artist whose Triple AAA audience put her on target for several hundred thousand records sold. In the world of multinational record labels, such an album is not worth the time and trouble when other "priorities" loom.

"I sat down on the couch for a couple days and bawled my eyes out, but then I decided, "okay, I'm going to throw a party," recalled Brooke. "So I had all my friends over who had been dropped by major labels: Wendy & Lisa, Michelle N'degocello. It was a big party. We commiserated, drank a bunch of wine and we thought, "Maybe we should all just get tattoos because this is an elite club. We're so cool. We've been dropped by a least two major labels each."

The next morning, the thought occurred to Brooke that there had to be a better way than moving from label to label for the rest of her career.

"I can sit around on my couch and be miserable and bitter," she thought. "Or I can do something. And I have to do something anyway because I have a tour to finish. So I'm going to have to get back out there and make my way."

Brooke's manager came up with an idea: record some of the remaining shows on the upcoming tour dates and release them as a live album, perhaps offering it first to some of her fans on the mailing list. Then, if sales were brisk, they could release it to stores.

"So we recorded a bunch of the next shows and the amazing thing was that as overwhelmed and daunted as I was by the fact that I had no label—my publishing company had just dropped me, too—nothing had changed," Brooke said. "My career was intact. My audiences were still filling up the theaters and clubs. They didn't give a shit whose logo was on the back of my CD jewel case. They wanted to see the show. They wanted to buy the music. It didn't matter whose *label* it was on."

Brooke said that realization was "incredibly empowering. "Like, wow, I'm alive. Nothing has changed. MCA didn't hurt this."

When *Jonatha Brooke Live* was released on her own Bad Dog Records, the artist and her manager were so pleased, they decided to expand their original plans. They built a web site, working hard to make it easy to navigate. They also created a place on the site for fans to talk about the record.

Then they hired their own publicist and began to promote two songs to Triple AAA radio stations. They also purchased promotional opportunities in several retail store programs that would offer prominent positioning in the stores and allow them to appear on the in-store listening booths programming.

"And it worked great," Brooke said. "It basically paid for itself."

Thus emboldened, Brooke went back in the studio to record a new album of original material, titled *Steady Pull*. This time, Brooke released her record as a DVD. She again worked the web site, publicity and radio angles.

The promotion again paid off. Her single, *My Song*, was a top five song at Triple AAA radio, and sales put Brooke at the forefront of the new breed of DIY artists emerging after careers at major record labels.

"I think I have a higher profile than I ever did before," said Brooke of her newfound career status. "I have gotten amazing press. I was able to do the Letterman show for the first time. That was such a dream come true. I think I could have died right then. We've started distributing my records in Ireland, Denmark and Sweden and I've started to tour in those countries."

Brooke also placed songs in the film, *Peter Pan* and on TV's *Dawson's Creek*.

"I feel like my career is at a better place than ever," Brooke said. "You know, all of this stuff is cumulative, and I think if you are out there long enough with integrity and doing something well and consistently, it just snowballs and eventually comes back to you."

Brooke was also realistic about her past experience.

"I really don't have any bitterness about the majors. I can't fault them. They have their own model and that's what they do. And I had no illusions about going into major label deals. I knew what I was getting into. And it would be a great luxury to have that kind of machinery behind me and that kind of money.

"But right now, what I'm doing is getting my music out there. Any number of artists that I adore and respect are trapped and nothing's happening for them and they can't move forward. So I'm incredibly lucky to be doing what I'm doing."

Four artists, four stories. The common thread is the desire to control their own destiny. But as we will see in the next chapter, even DIY'ing requires adherence to certain rules.

HOW NOT TO RUIN YOUR MUSIC CAREER

1. Be realistic about your choices.
2. Persistence is your key asset.

3
THE RULES OF THE GAME

Success has many fathers, but failure is an orphan, goes an old Chinese saying. How true that is for the recording business. When a record is successful (i.e., has sold over 1,000,000 copies, the level for attaining "platinum" status in industry certifications), there is a long, grey line of executives slapping each other on the back and taking credit for the success.

An album stiffs? The finger-pointing starts and people quietly start distancing themselves from the project.

The executive turnover in the upper levels of the major record industry is astounding, given its status as a multinational, billion-dollar business. Most of the top executives at major record labels have worked for two or three other record companies in their career. Many have worked for even more, shuffling between jobs in the old boys and girls network.

The reasons behind the excessive turnover of employees have elements familiar to any corporate situation: burnout, personality conflicts, poor performance. It also has aspects unique to this sector of the entertainment business—a combination of the high stakes and the unlikely prospects for success.

With most record albums failing to attain the sales level necessary to sustain the large overhead and make a profit for the multinational corporations, label executives need at least one of their priority releases to sell an astonishing number of records in order to salvage the failures.

There is typically a three-year window of opportunity for those same executives to prove themselves worthy of their job and its enormous perks. Sometimes, the time frame is even less.

In the modern record industry, there is a better than even chance that the person who signs you to a major record label (i.e., one owned by a multinational corporation) and the executive team surrounding her/him will not be supervising your ultimate release. Thus, signing away a lifetime of rights on the basis of a personal relationship with anyone is not a good idea.

This is not to suggest that smaller independent labels have much of an advantage over major recording companies. The employee turnover ratio at many of those labels is often equally high, in some cases because of the low level of wages and the mercurial personalities of the entrepreneurs that founded those companies.

But the turnover happens mostly because the business practices at an independent record label follow the same rule as a large major label—sales must sustain overhead. While independents are typically better at keeping overhead lower and working more closely with a smaller number of acts, things can and do fall through the cracks.

With that in mind, we advise anyone aspiring to success in the record industry to pay attention to the following rules, listed in no particular order, that constitute the **ten magic laws of life as a recording artist.**

Understanding them may not lead to success, but certainly will help cushion possible disappointments along your career path.

 GOODNESS HAS NOTHING TO DO WITH IT: You can be the world's finest musician and you may not achieve any success because of luck, timing or any number of factors that are out of your control. Talent is often subjective, and what one person deems genius is a joke to another. When judgments are being passed on something you've worked hard to create and hold dear, it's going to be tough to deal with the emotional highs and lows. Particularly in times when the financial rewards are often not great.

2 **STICK WITH YOUR VISION**: Be prepared to stick to your artistic vision. There are all sorts of wacky ideas that various people who purport to have some sort of industry expertise will suggest along the way (present company excluded, of course!). You should be extremely wary of altering your core vision of who you are and what you represent. Remember when Billy Squier, a toast of the heavy metal world, made a video where he was crawling on all fours and prancing across his bedroom? The move was career suicide. Someone, somewhere probably suggested that it was a good idea to do it, just as someone encouraged Liz Phair to abandon her fan base and credibility in a bid to become a commercial artist or said it was okay for the cameras to be rolling while Metallica worked on its therapy. Remember this when you're confronted with similar inane suggestions. If you're going to go down in career flames, at least have your hand on the controls.

3 **THE ONLY INTEREST IS SELF-INTEREST**: Many of the various advisors (who will assure you that they are watching out for your interests) are probably more concerned with the interest they're drawing on the money you're earning. Remember that agents, managers, accountants, attorneys and many other water carriers of the recording business are typically paid upfront on the gross amount of any deal they negotiate. If you sign away the rights to your artistic achievement, be aware that you are mortgaging your future and that some of your advisors may be more interested in getting as much money as they can upfront than ensuring that your rights are protected.

4 **DIVISION OF LABOR:** If you are part of a group, the same rules apply to the growth of the enterprise as would apply to starting a hardware store. In other words, there needs to be someone watching the store at all times and the duties of each partner need to be clearly and completely outlined. Much as you would be upset if you had to re-stock the shelves at the hardware store by yourself while your partner spends time with his girlfriend, so, too, will you be upset if someone constantly skips rehearsal because of a personal commitment. The window of opportunity for your career's success is way too short to be involved with someone who will not give absolute commitment to a project. No matter how talented someone may be, enterprises rise and fall on the actual work of the participants, not potential.

5 **YOU'RE ALWAYS DOING IT YOURSELF, EVEN WHEN OTHERS ARE SUPPOSEDLY DOING IT FOR YOU:** This goes hand-in-glove with rule No. 3. You have to keep a constant eye out for yourself and do all the little steps involved in managing an enterprise, even when there purportedly are people who are doing it for you. This is whether you're working with a major or independent company or a handful of outside specialists. You have to ask questions, badger, follow-up and do your own math. When you hire someone, you are delegating authority, not abrogating it. Ask for weekly reports on progress.

6 **IT'S NOT THE GROSS, IT'S THE NET:** No matter how much money you are offered, you have to break down the deal and see how much of the bottom line will be put in your pocket. There's a reason why many major record labels need to sell one million CDs before they can consider a particular campaign a success. A huge advance is recoupable, which means you will be using that money for all your expenses before additional funds arrive.

7 **BE KIND TO THE PEOPLE YOU MEET ON THE WAY UP**: Believe it or not, the vast, worldwide recorded music industry is a very, very tiny place. Particularly with the instantaneous power of the Internet, being a jerk to a soundman, waitress or roadies will come back to bite you in the crotch. While most of you will show kindness and compassion to everyone you meet along the way, we all have our bad days. That's when you need to exert the utmost discretion and control to keep a lid on your anger.

8 **THE GOAL IS TO BE A WORLDWIDE STAR**: It is, and it isn't. If you're like most creative people, your goal should be to keep creating art and making a comfortable living doing so. Would you be happy to be a one-hit wonder? Many tales abound of the musician who had the one moment of glory and is now back waiting tables in the tiny village he or she once abandoned and scorned. Everything that's fun about life in the creative world—including sex, drugs and rock 'n roll—can be stretched out over the years with the right career vision.

9 **NEVER JOIN A TRIO WITH A HUSBAND AND WIFE**: It goes without saying that blood runs thicker than water. When you enter into situations where your input and control are not valued, you will soon grow disenchanted. Seek out situations that empower you and your creative spirit, not grind you down.

10 **THERE'S AN EXCEPTION TO EVERY RULE**: And it all goes back to talent and creative vision. Don't live in someone else's vision of your success. Live in your own.

HOW NOT TO RUIN YOUR MUSIC CAREER

1. Remember that the worldwide recording industry is run by human beings.

2. Keep in mind that you are always in charge of your career, no matter what others tell you.

3. Understand that you will have to live with the consequences of any artistic decisions, so make them yourself.

4
INDIE, MAJOR OR DIY

There are three paths to music success for anyone looking to carve out a career. All rely on a basic business premise: you must create multiple ways to sell an individual or group's music and music-related products to others, including through recorded music, live gigs, merchandising, licensing, publishing, online and through subscriptions.

Some of these paths require you to give up control of your music for all time in return for help in achieving that goal. Others allow more control, but less access to the huge star-making machinery of the worldwide music industry.

Only you can determine what's most important to you. And, let's face it, most people, if offered an obscene amount of money up front, are likely to leap at it. That's human nature. It's also akin to rolling the dice at the casino, except it's your artistic life at stake.

Because even if you win, the returns aren't nearly as great as you would believe.

Steve Albini, a producer for Nirvana, is the author of *The Problem with Music*, an infamous diatribe against record company accounting that has circled the Internet for years.

In his epistle, Albini said he always imagines a band about to sign with a major label in the following context:

"I imagine a trench, about four feet wide and five feet deep, maybe sixty yards long, filled with runny, decaying shit. I imagine these people, some of them good friends, some of them barely acquaintances, at one end of this trench. I also imagine a faceless industry lackey at the other end holding a fountain pen and a contract waiting to be signed."

Albini goes on to detail the results of a band that has an album out on an independent label that gets a $250,000 advance to sign with a major.

The result? After every attorney, accountant, manager and associate is paid, the band's $250,000 results in each member of an imaginary three-piece band netting slightly over $4,000.

The moral of the story is that it's not how much you gross, but how much you net after everyone is paid.

It's not how much you gross, but how much you net after everyone is paid.

Huge advances come with huge expenses. Remember, an advance is just that—it's a payout in ADVANCE of record sales. From that, you have to pay everyone in your employ and embark on a series of costly promotional activities that will also entail considerable money out of your own pocket.

The long-term value of your career lies in controlling the fruits of your labor, i.e., your songwriting and master recordings. Long after you've stopped touring, these are the enduring legacies of your work and can generate substantial revenue.

You can be paid directly from that revenue stream if you're savvy about setting up your career in the proper way. Or you can take an accountant's word for it at your record company. An audit of said accountant's bookkeeping will often cost upwards of $50,000, making it cost-prohibitive for many artists.

It is usually only in hindsight that an artist realizes what they have surrendered.

The artist known as Seven is an extremely active musician/composer in Hollywood, perhaps best known for writing the theme song to *The Simple Life*, the Paris Hilton reality TV show.

After signing a deal with a major, he later rued his mistake.

"I took a passenger seat instead of the ambitious driver seat," he said. "What you need to do is to have a full team, a full plan and a business working underneath you, selling your CDs, having merchandise set up, building bases, starting in your own area, and building it out little by little across your own county. When I got to the record label, I was so exhausted (by that activity), it was like, 'I finally got here, please help me.' I thought everybody was just going to do it all for me."

What Seven soon discovered—as do most artists—is that you are ALWAYS out there on your own, even with a support team in place. You have to monitor the activities of the small business you are creating, analyzing cost versus benefit, always understanding the commitments that are being made in your name and particularly monitoring the revenue streams that are derived from your hard work.

Doing-it-yourself (hereafter referred to as DIY) is how virtually everyone in the entertainment business started their career. Rare is the individual who was "discovered" and vaulted to the top without paying dues.

DIY has a broad interpretation, and certainly doesn't mean doing every last bit of work necessary to launch your career by yourself. What it does mean is taking the time to properly plan each step of the process and enlisting the proper outside help where necessary.

DIY means that you have taken responsibility for the success and failure of your own career. You will typically record the music yourself, design the artwork for the package, book your own gigs, work on your marketing, promotion and publicity and generally guide the process.

Many artists complain that doing everything in their business relationships hurts their creative side. This left brain/right brain conundrum is the reason that many opt for signing with a record company, hoping that allowing that corporation to take charge of the basic tasks will free their creative spirit to concentrate on the fun tasks of the business, songwriting and performing.

The fallacy of that argument is that most artists are still doing it themselves, even though they've signed away the rights to their music in return for an advance and royalties. Yes, despite the golden promises extended as an inducement to sign the contracts, the over-worked staff at most record companies will still need the involvement and assistance of the artist in order to fulfill most of their tasks.

Remember when you sign those deals: in many cases, the ever-shifting employment of record company staffers and the fast-changing whims of the public create orphaned acts whose backers have fled and whose prospects are dim. It's not unusual to have an album shelved, which means your music is in commercial limbo, not eligible for release and never heard by the public—and, also, not earning anything for you.

Despite the golden promises at the contract signing, you will be faced with some unpleasant choices, which can include abandoning your songs and master recordings. In some cases, the contract you signed may be particularly egregious, requiring you to sign away rights to your band's name and Internet URL. You will not be able to continue a music career using that identity, because you no longer own it. It belongs to the company that signed you.

Life for even the major label musician is filled with hard, do-it-yourself work. The same principles that help the do-it-yourself band achieve success are the ones that make the major label band work.

There are the radio interviews at 6 a.m., in-store appearances at noon, a marketing meeting at 3 p.m., followed by glad-handing of staffers and a show at night. Do that in every city while touring the country and it's no wonder you'll soon be throwing objects out of the hotel room window (reminder: that's not a recoupable expense).

There will always be someone to tell you what to do, when you have to show up, what can be on your record, what can be on your video, who you have to talk to and when. You can't push that off on someone else. That's the cold, hard truth.

In the world of the musician, the upfront money is always the carrot on the stick to success. Take the money and then let tomorrow be damned is the typical attitude, usually based on the assumption that success is so momentary and fleeting that capitalizing on the heat of the moment is the proper recourse.

David Baram is the president of the Firm, a management company which handles Linkin Park, Limp Bizkit and many other top musicians and actors. In a Harvard Law School forum held in April 2004,

Baram acknowledged that careers have a limited window at the upper levels.

"Entertainment is a very short term, frustrating business, here today/gone tomorrow," said Baram. "I don't know who you are all listening to now, but odds are none of it will be relevant three or four years from now."

While that's true to an extent, what Baram was referring to is a career at the very top of the charts. Even those musicians who are no longer "relevant" can still carve out a decent career from touring, merchandising and creating new music to a smaller, core audience of fans. Just look at the concert schedules of any summer fairs and or 5,000-seat venue and you'll see that most of the artists performing at those locations have been around forever. Hardly any still have a major label recording contract.

Many of those acts no longer hold the rights to the recordings that made them successful. And while it's arguable that a great deal, if not all, of those acts owe their success to the marketing and promotion they received as part of their record deal, it's also true that many of them are now making more money than they ever did. Why? Because most of them have learned that they should control as much of their revenue stream as possible, including new recordings, merchandise and tour revenues.

> **Today's musician negotiates from strength. Having attained a fan base and sales on their own, they can determine what rights they will surrender contractually and under what terms.**

As the commercial music industry begins to change, owning the rights to your revenue streams becomes a tempting target for the larger companies. Contracts that once merely sought rights to recordings now look for everything from a band's image to its merchandising to its Internet URL.

While the advances offered under such deals may be even larger than previous generations, be sure that they are even deadlier than the old-time deals that offered the bucket of chicken and a new car. An artist that does not control their own Internet address or image is out of business if the record company locks them up. While an artist can tour without a recording, it's impossible to tour without your own name.

In an ever-changing commercial music industry, many successful acts opt to build up their track record before consigning their music to individual record companies. Sales of 10,000 units and above usually indicate a reliable fan base for the music, which in turn may translate into even bigger sales with some added marketing, promotion and publicity muscle.

The key difference is that today's musician negotiates from strength. Having attained a fan base and sales on their own, they can determine what rights they will surrender contractually and under what terms.

While many record companies today are demanding income from music publishing, merchandising and other revenues, it is not uncommon for bands to merely license their music for a limited duration for distribution, with all rights reverting back to the artist once that limited term is fulfilled.

The in-vogue term for this process is "upstreaming," which refers to a deal in which an act on an independent record label moves to a major label after a certain sales level has been reached. In return, the independent label receives distribution and other marketing incentives.

Many major record labels actually prefer this method of dealing with a new act. One, it eliminates the guesswork associated with a raw label act. Instead of spending huge amounts of money upfront and guessing whether an act will be viable, it now has an established track record of success and a working model of the group's fan base.

Since multinational record companies generally run on three-year cycles, which is roughly equivalent to the amount of time it takes for a slate of albums by the artist roster to be released and vetted by the consumer marketplace, many opt for contracts that tie up an act's master recordings for roughly twice that length, or six years.

As with any deal, keep in mind that if the expenses used to boost record sales results in overall lower profits, or if the expected hits fail to emerge, then the executive team is often shuffled. Which could mean that your project will be placed on the back-burner by the incoming regime, who, after all, have their own priorities and will not be eager to make someone else look good by boosting up an artist for which they will have to share the credit.

Even with a limited time contract, it is not easy to just take your music and go elsewhere without a costly series of buyouts from your contract. That is, if the corporation would even consider such a buy-out. Nothing makes a label look worse than seeing an act flee to another company and have success. Further, it is better to shelve an album, locking up your music in a storage vault for eternity.

Another consideration in any prospective deal is whether the financial stability of the company will allow it to live up to its marketing and promotional guarantees.

Every record company has priorities. There are acts that will be given the full push at radio, retail, through publicity and online. If a company has just experienced a few bad fiscal quarters, it will have to lower the number of albums it can plug to the various sales channels. That could mean that your album receives less attention than it deserves.

If you are signed to an imprint of the main label, it also could mean that your album receives less attention. Imagine the dilemma of the person plugging the album to retail and radio. Both sides want to know that the record company is backing albums to the full extent.

In retail's case, that means the record company will devote money to what's known as price and positioning, i.e., the posters and standees and other attention-grabbers that stores sell to manufacturers anxious to get a shopper to buy their products.

For radio, they want to know how much attention is being paid to the record by the various other divisions. And, in modern times, whether the record company will take out paid advertisements that will allow the station to play the song over and over and over in those hard-to-fill hours of the evening, or offer the radio station executives other perks.

The people pushing the albums have a limited number of priorities. They can't go to these outlets and tell them they have ten great records coming out next week. No, it's a matter of priorities; they will push two and, perhaps, talk about ten others.

In the end, every musician is either at the mercy of larger powers that be or doing it themselves. The most successful acts are those that keep on top of their business every step of the way. Knowing your options is the most important factor in determining which path you will choose.

HOW NOT TO RUIN YOUR MUSIC CAREER

1. Keep in mind that the net profit you will reap is the most important consideration in weighing any deal.

2. Record executives come and go. Do not sign any deal based strictly on personal relationships.

3. The shorter the term, the better. In today's music industry, the market changes fast.

4. Negotiate. Make a counter-offer on any proposal.

5
ORGANIZATIONS AND NETWORKING

Even the person who is doing it themselves needs sounding boards in the business. The arts are like any other business—people like to do business with people they like. Thus, it should be your goal to meet and befriend as many people who work in the arts as possible, for these connections will serve you well in all aspects of your career.

In old school record industry thinking, this used to mean you had to be in New York, Nashville and Los Angeles (or London or another major international capital, depending on your desire), because that's where the business was conducted.

After the regional businesses of the early years of the recorded music business faded, everything was centralized, with decisions flowing out of the home offices of the multinational recording labels.

Bright-eyed individuals got off the buses in New York, Nashville, et al with their guitars slung over their shoulders, hoping to make an impact on the people in these major hubs whose opinions could get them "signed" to a deal.

Occasionally, regional scenes would revive and flourish, then be cherry-picked by labels and die again.

Today, thanks to the power of e-mail and the reawakening of the musician to the reality that building a business that lasts starts regionally, the music scene of the moment is anywhere a musician happens to be.

Information on manufacturing, distribution, marketing and other phases of the industry is available 24/7 at the speed of a Google. When more information or face-to-face meetings are needed, there are regional conferences and seminars run by national and local organizations, giving musicians the ability to network and meet others who are dealing with the same creative and business issues that they are.

The record industry owned by major entertainment conglomcrates is gradually switching to a model where a handful of superstars are marketed and promoted across a variety of platforms. Thanks to the wonders of auto tuning and other studio tricks, it doesn't even matter anymore whether an artist is particularly musical. They can patch together virtually anything and make it sound good. Any number of wonderful teen talents have had the fortunate privilege of dealing with such a star system.

That leaves the independent world, filling up the market void of the other 95 percent of the business. The independent doesn't have money for videos, big radio, huge promotional campaigns at retail and all the millions of things that go into a major star's campaign. But they do have the advantage of creating a smaller, more intimate, one-to-one experience that has any number of possible offshoots. You can create a multi-media empire, as many artists do. Jane Siberry does salons; Delbert McClinton has cruises; Jim Roll writes books; others are content running their own record companies and concentrating on songwriting.

Even in your own little insular, artistic world, it helps to occasionally get out of the house and network. There are, ahem, the many fine DIY Conventions that are held in various parts of the U.S. and abroad. Keep track of the upcoming events at www.diyconvention.com.

There's also the National Association of Record Industry Professionals, a membership organization devoted to furthering education and networking among those interested in making a career in the record industry. Find out more at NARIP.com.

Another organization to consider is the National Academy of Recording Arts & Sciences, the fine folks who put on the Grammys each year. Although heavily skewed to the major record labels, they do put on many fine educational events through their various regional chapters. Find out more at NARA.org.

If you have an interest in the digital music space, there are informal gatherings in many cities of a group known as Pho, after the Vietnamese soup that was consumed at the first gathering and then at subsequent meetings in cities that have Vietnamese restaurants. The Pho.org web site has details about signing up for its mailing list.

Many national music-centric conventions have developed over the last decade, bringing together musicians from various regions of the country for education, networking, and showcasing opportunities.

South by Southwest (or SXSW, its well-known abbreviation) is one of the best-known events. Held each March in Austin, Texas, the live music capital of the world, the event is informally known as the music industry's Spring break. The voluminous nightclubs of Austin offer a week's worth of showcases from a selection of local, regional, national, and international bands, as selected by the convention's programmers.

The event has become so popular and huge that it has spawned a number of unsanctioned guerilla parties around the Austin area.

The annual CMJ Music Marathon, sponsored by the College Media Journal, is held each fall in New York City. Once focused exclusively on college radio and its needs, the convention has mushroomed to embrace all aspects of the record industry, from DIY to majors, and offers a full run of music showcases in New York clubs.

2NMC is Nashville's largest convention, and the Independent Music Conference (IMC) has taken over Philadelphia for the last two years. Also of note are such regional affairs as MusicFest NW in Portland, the Future of Music Convention in Washington, D.C., and Nadine Condon's Nadine's Wild Weekend in San Francisco.

Your best bet in choosing such conferences, which in some cases can cost hundreds of dollars, is to pick and choose which ones best serve your personal budget, growth and interests of the moment.

At the least, all of the above offer excellent educational and schmoozing opportunities.

Unfortunately, while there are many high-minded and interesting organizations in the world, there are also predators looking to separate the unwary from their bankrolls. The promise of these somewhat sneaky and snarky groups is very old school and designed to lure people who think getting "signed" is the way to go.

These organizations also advertise that they have some magic, hidden access to artist and repertoire people and other major label affiliates that are seeking new music. They offer to set up showcases in front of these music industry professionals, sometimes charging hundreds of dollars for that privilege. Then, the showcase winds up being in front of a few employees of said service, which quickly packs up and moves on to the next city.

HOW NOT TO RUIN YOUR MUSIC CAREER

1. Get out and network, network, network.
2. Be wary of conventions and services that promise access to A&R.
3. Don't move just to further your career.

6
SETTING UP SUCCESS

Make no mistake; setting up your career in music is like setting up any small business. Sure, you need to have talent and songwriting skills and the ability to play an instrument or sing. But a business mistake made at the very beginning of your career could be one that you'll regret until the end of it.

The best method of making sure you are aligning your stars properly is to start off by writing a business plan. A business plan is a map of where you see your business at its start and where you believe it is heading. The document outlines your plans for sales, advertising, promotion, marketing and financing.

Wait! Don't run for the door or the next chapter. It's not that hard to compose a business plan. And it will point out some of the fatal flaws in your plan for world domination, or at least let you know how much money you'll need to raise to get off the ground in your new venture.

Without a business plan most ventures lurch along and, perhaps, stumble into success. But the business we're advising you to set up in this book is different from the old system of music sales. This one requires you to actually plan your expenditures and set some goals.

While some short-sighted individuals may scoff at the notion that you can plan for success in the arts, having financial goals and a schedule to achieve those goals will probably get you to your dream sooner than a random, haphazard and ill-conceived stab at selling music.

First, you must take care of formally setting up your business. If you are a solo musician, you can set up what is known as a sole proprietorship. The advantage of creating this entity is that it requires very little paperwork. The downside is that if your business gets into trouble, you can be sued personally and your debtors can recover from your personal assets, including your home, car and personal bank accounts.

The other big danger to this business construct is that, if you have any employees, they can sue you if they are injured on the job. A strained back lifting an amp, a fight between a roadie and a townie, an accident on the way to a gig—all can result in you being personally liable for whatever results.

> Having financial goals and a schedule to achieve those goals will probably get you to your dream sooner than a random, haphazard and ill-conceived stab at selling music.

But as a sole proprietor, you do not need to file a separate business tax return. Just add a Schedule C form to your own personal 1040 and you're good to go. Your business income and other personal income are combined and taxed at your personal income tax rate.

All businesses must obtain what is known as an employee identification number, or EIN. If you are a sole proprietor, you can use your own Social Security Number as your EIN. The number is free and can be obtained from the Internal Revenue Service by requesting a SS-4 form.

A partnership is another route to consider when establishing a business. A general partnership is conceived when two or more people are aiming to open a for-profit business.

A general partnership can be formed either orally or (preferably) in writing. However, without any agreement, someone who leaves the business can claim an interest in it at a later time, possibly leading to a lawsuit. Thus, spelling out rights and responsibilities is the safest route, particularly in the volatile field of creative endeavors.

With a general partnership, each partner helps to run the day-to-day business and contributes an equal amount of cash or services in exchange for their interest. Each partner has equal authority for running it. That means that anyone can represent the partners and make business decisions that will be binding on all of them.

You have a duty under a partnership to treat your partners fairly and exhibit loyalty to them. You must avoid conflicts of interest, such as competing with the existing business. Partners share in the profit and losses of the business and report their share of same on their personal income taxes.

The major downside to this arrangement is that each partner has unlimited personal liability stemming from the actions of the other. Even if you didn't know or approve of the other partner's actions, you can still be liable for the results.

A corporation is a legal entity that is separate from the individuals who own it. The shareholders are the people who invest money in the company and are given shares of corporate stock. By owning those shares, they have the right to participate in business decisions and receive dividends from the company.

You can have either a public or a private corporation. A private corporate can have stock held by one individual or several. Public corporations are generally larger and most are publicly available for purchase via a stock exchange.

A corporation shareholder has personal liability, but is limited to only the money invested in the corporation. Your personal assets cannot be attached to cover the debts of the corporation, unless you have personally guaranteed those debts.

In this kind of tax setup, the corporation pays taxes separately from its owners, who, in turn, pay personal taxes on any wages or dividends they receive from the corporation.

If you have partners in your enterprise (which is what the other people in the band are, no matter if they are lifelong friends or someone you just met), you need to create a partnership agreement, corporate entity or limited liability company that will articulate the rights and responsibilities of each individual.

The reason? Just by two people coming together and sharing in the profits and losses of a company, you already are in a partnership, whether you know it or not. In case of a dispute, state partnership law is going to determine how your assets are going to be broken up between members. Typically, that can get very ugly very quickly.

Here's one example of things going terribly wrong without an agreement: the drummer who sat in the room while you and your bass player composed a hit song that made millions? He or she is entitled to a share in the songwriting.

Another? When you go into the studio and the producer changes the chorus or adds a bridge, the producer is entitled to a percentage of the song. Again, he or she is in the room and aides in the writing of the song, and therefore is entitled to a percentage.

It's always advisable to keep a record of the plans, even at the very beginning.

"You can jot it down on a piece of paper and it'll probably make sense to somebody, or you can talk about it into a tape recorder and people can keep a handle on it," according to Neville Johnson, a Los Angeles based entertainment attorney. "I had a very nasty piece of litigation involving a group called Better Than Ezra, which didn't take care of business on that level and it got into a hairy, hairy expensive lawsuit, and it's not uncommon."

There is a lot at stake in this, even at the very beginning. So, while no one likes to sit down and hassle with the legal aspects of dividing up the pie, it's very much a necessary step in the process. It's what separates the people who are just doing it for kicks from the people who are attempting to develop a serious career and business. You must decide such basic issues as who owns the group name, who controls the name, who the managing partner is, and how the profits and songwriting credits will be split.

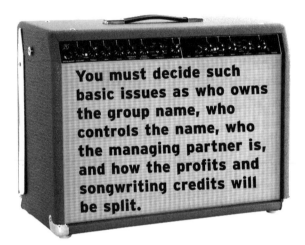

You must decide such basic issues as who owns the group name, who controls the name, who the managing partner is, and how the profits and songwriting credits will be split.

We all know the counter-argument. Oh, so-and-so never did that. They were an artist who concentrated on her or his art. They made millions of dollars and had worldwide success.

Frankly, being cheated is being cheated, no matter what level of the business you're on. Steven Ames Brown, an attorney who specializes in royalty recovery, once noted that he had never seen an audit of a record company account that did not uncover some money. The problem is that such audits cost $50,000 and up, well beyond the means of most artists.

And need we point out the long string of successful musicians who wound up suing their managers and agents and accountants once they discovered how much more money they would have made with a proper system of accountability in place?

Two additional words of caution: you may want to retain your own attorney to look over any agreement, rather than relying on one attorney to cover the group. Majority rules is not always the best for an individual.

And an oral agreement? Sam Goldwin said it best: it's not worth the paper it's written on. Although technically it's just as binding as a written contract, you'll have big problems proving it.

A good deal of the forms you need to start your partnership can be found online. Nolo.com or Incorporate.com are great sources for available forms. The various state governments also have forms for downloading. Fees vary from state to state, but are typically a few hundred dollars.

When you set up your new company, you can choose to do so as a for-profit corporation, or a not-for-profit, which is generally used by religious, charitable, educational and other organizations.

A corporation is generally set up to limit the personal liability of its owners. We live in a litigious society, so it's best to prepare for the grim day when someone will crawl out of the woodwork and attempt to sue the beejeezus out of you.

On the plus side, ambitious people can also set up a corporation to sell stocks or bonds, thus raising more money.

Most musicians will consider starting what's known as a Limited Liability Company, which has most of the advantages of starting a corporation but is taxed differently. You can also start a General Partnership, which is what two or more persons form when they are engaged in a business for profit. Your profits are taxed as personal income for the partners.

When considering your options, consult an attorney to receive advice on which is best for your situation.

The performing rights organization (or PRO, as the acronym is widely known) is another initial consideration. These are the organizations that account for a great deal of the money dispensed to publishers and songwriters.

In the United States, the three PROs are the American Society of Composers, Authors and Publishers (ASCAP), Broadcast Music Inc. (BMI) and SESAC, which once had a name to go along with its acronym, but now just goes by its initials.

The very basic function of these organizations is to monitor and collect performance royalties that come in from film, television, radio and live performances of your music. But they also serve as multi-faceted educational organizations and have a good deal of out-reach into various aspects of the music industry community.

A performance rights organization is in charge of getting you paid if someone is using your music in a public performance. That means if a radio station in New York or a barbershop in Peoria is playing a song that you've written, you will ostensibly be part of the collective performance pool of money derived from licensing such organizations and receive some money based on an allocation formula.

Which PRO is right for you? That's a subjective decision. All of them have major web sites that detail the benefits of joining their particular organizations. Most musicians feel that the personal interaction that they have with their representative is the determining factor in which organization gets your collection assignment.

PRO staffs are typically much more stable than record or publishing companies. The representative you click with is likely to be on board for a number of years.

Even after you join a PRO and decide that it's not for you, you can switch your affiliation or decide to set up another publishing company under the dominion of the other organization.

"I went exclusively off of the feel that I was getting from the representative; whether or not I felt that he was going to be there when I needed some questions answered, and whether or not I could call and get some information from them," said Bobby Borg, drummer for the multi-platinum band Warrant, talking about his decision.

It's never too soon to join these organizations, as they are extremely helpful to members early in their careers, serving as much as a counselor on the business as a collection agency.

A copyright is a protection provided by the government that prevents someone from stealing or otherwise exploiting your composition or creation without your permission.

Your work becomes copyrighted as soon as you transform an original idea into some sort of tangible form, whether that is lyrics on a sheet of paper or a music song idea on a cassette recorder.

There is a common misconception among young musicians that you have to actually put something in the mail and register it in order to have copyright protection. While that is highly advisable to back up your claims, a copyright already exists and grants you exclusive rights to your work at the moment it is put into tangible form.

Because the bottom line in any dispute is that you have to be able to show that your work is YOUR work, it is advisable to do the paperwork to back up your claims. The copyright process is a good mechanism to do that.

Particularly in cases where your music is going to be published and exploited in some way for commercial sale, you want to be protected. That's when you file the form and register it with those folks in Washington, D.C. at the copyright office. Doing so gives you the reputable presumption that you are the author and owner of that composition and it gives you the right to file an infringement claim. You will get a registration number which is proof on what you sent in at that time.

That means, of course, that someone may come along later and say, "Hey, I wrote *Jumpin' Jack Flash*" and claim to own the song. You will then have to prove your authorship if it comes up in a court of law.

Although many musicians fear that someone will steal their song, outright theft happens much less than you would think.

"It's not that common," said David Moser, an author on music copyright. "It does happen, certainly, on occasion, but not nearly as frequently as most people assume. One of the problems is that there are a lot of similarities in different creative works that occur. It's real easy for two people to write a song independently of each other and there will be similarities in those two songs. Those things happen by sheer coincidence, most of the time."

Copyright law never protects an idea. You cannot copyright an idea. What you can copyright is the way you express an idea.

If you have an idea for a song about two people falling in love, you can't copyright that idea. But if you write a song that details specific facts about the two people falling in love, you can protect it.

The so-called "poor man's copyright" is a popular way to protect your work, however, it's not foolproof.

In this method, someone takes a copy of their work, sticks it in an envelope and mails it to himself or herself. They leave the envelope sealed, thereby getting a time stamped and dated affirmation that the work was in existence at a particular moment.

Unfortunately, the determination on the validity of copyright by that method would be up to a judge, who will determine whether the envelope remained sealed during the period you claim that it was.

A copyright form is available online and costs $30. If you feel your work has value, it is money well spent.

A trademark is another consideration. It depends on what time it is in your career, and what exactly you want to protect. The USPTO.gov site can give you the details; a lawyer can explain them.

Essentially, when you're playing regionally, you own the rights for that trademark in that geographic region. If you get signed, you have to do a federal search, and that's when you may discover a band in Louisiana who has the same name and problems might come up. The search costs a few hundred dollars.

Generally, if someone is using your copyright or trademark without your permission, you need to send them a letter and demand that they stop. Particularly in the age of the Internet, many people do not know that something they find online cannot be used without permission.

Once you're square with copyrighting your work, it's time to consider the place you're going to be performing the arduous task of creating said work in. For a great majority of creative people in this day and age, that's the home. You set up a home recording studio, a desk in the corner for paperwork, and that's the office.

But, of course, it's never that easy. Home-based businesses are taxed by many cities as well as the state and federal government, and many of them want you to register your business with them and, in some cases, obtain a permit.

The zoning permit says you can do the business that you are doing in your home. In most cases, they don't want that business to be very loud. They don't want you to use heavy machinery. And they certainly don't want a lot of foot traffic.

When you are applying for your business permit and you are working out of your home recording an album, it's probably best to say that you are working with headphones and direct recording, producing little noise and very little foot traffic.

Licensing your business through the city should not be much of a hassle. Ultimately, no city can stop you from conducting a legal business that doesn't interfere with your neighbor's right to the quiet enjoyment of their domicile. Your registration is mostly concerned with making sure the city gets its tax share of any revenue generated.

Capital is typically needed to start up any business. Most musicians will already own their own instruments, so the rest of the potential costs may include opening up a PO Box, paying the attorney and/or accountant fees to get the business properly set up, purchasing a home computer, and squirreling away a little money for various miscellaneous expenses related to your career.

Although the cost of recording an album has plummeted, there's still the need to either record the album at a studio or buy home recording equipment to get the project done. Some innovative musicians have gone to extraordinary lengths in outside-the-box thinking to overcome limited cash.

One great example of getting the funds to do it yourself was the route taken by Grey Eye Glances, an East Coast band that decided to do its own recording.

Grey Eye Glances had been through the recording industry mill when it got the idea to create an album entirely funded by its fan base.

The band was one of the victims of the giant merger between Universal Music and PolyGram in the late 1990s, which saw many music acts dropped when the rosters of the two huge companies were combined. Grey Eye Glances' Mercury Records home base was one of the most severely affected labels in that merger, and Grey Eye Glances was one of the acts dropped. They were left out in the cold without ownership of their master recordings.

A brief dabble with an East Coast company that wanted to make Grey Eye Glances the flagship act of a new label went nowhere, leaving the band to ponder its next move.

Realizing that no one understood Grey Eye Glances business prospects as well as its members, they decided to take the time-honored DIY route and formed Sojourn Hill Records, a label dedicated to their own music.

But then inspiration struck. Why carry the financial burden of creating that company yourself when it can be shared by the people who care most about the band's music?

Thus was born a limited liability company called "The Grey Album LLC." It was a vehicle whose sole mission was to fund the recording, manufacturing, marketing and distribution of a new Grey Eye Glances compact disc.

"Everybody can make a CD and everybody can borrow money and have mom and dad sign a collateralized loan," said Eric O'Dell, the bassist for Grey Eye Glances. "But that's not what we wanted to do. We thought we had a viable option for our business. So we approached people and asked them, "How would you like to become a part owner of an album?"

There are strict government rules on such solicitations. For one, you can't just post a note on the Internet and ask for blind donations. You have to formally prepare a business plan and approach individuals one-on-one, getting them to sign off on the investment opportunity.

Although the band had experience in running itself for years, they were in entirely new territory when they solicited the money needed to fund the new venture.

O'Dell used rough demos of the potential album's songs to entice his investors. "We mainly approached people who had bought a lot of stuff from us before," he said. "We had put out some unreleased music and sold it at $100 a pop to get our masters back from Mercury, so we went to the people who put the most money in there.

We were able to get about 40 people to step up, well-heeled fans who were in it for the love of our music."

The investors included doctors, attorneys, dentists, friends and relatives. They became silent partners in the limited liability company, with the band members serving as the managing directors.

A few months after getting its funds, the band released its album, *A Little Voodoo.*

One interesting method of raising money that some sophisticated DIY'ers with a bit of money have attempted is the so-called "reverse merger."

Basically, a reverse merger occurs when a private company merges with a public company that has no assets or liabilities. In general, it's a company that has basically gone out of business with its corporate structure its only asset. By merging into such an entity, a private company becomes a public company.

The advantage is that a private company becomes public at a lesser cost and can raise money by selling stock to outside investors, and can make acquisitions of other companies using the company's stock.

Of course, by becoming a public company, you are subject to additional scrutiny from the Securities and Exchange Commission. If you say you're going to release an album and will invest a certain amount of money to promote that album, you have to do it. Otherwise, it's illegal. Consult an accountant or other financial advisor for the details.

Another important item to consider when starting your business: health insurance.

Many struggling young music artists will be working a day job, which may include health benefits with a co-payment of as little as

$10 per month. But others may be working a job where health is not covered, or may not be working at all.

It's a big mistake to overlook this insurance. When you're young and full of energy, the last consideration is that you might wind up injured or too sick to work. But it happens. You can be hit by a truck and find yourself facing hundreds of thousands of dollars in medical bills after just a short hospital stay. The PROs have a health plan that offers insurance to musicians. You're strongly urged to take advantage.

In some states, there is a state disability fund that deducts money directly from an employee's paycheck that will pay a certain percentage of your salary if you are too sick or injured to work.

Taxes are an inevitable part of dealing with your business. Here's the good news: as a musician, you have a side business that allows you to deduct an enormous amount of things from your gross income.

Now is the time to start thinking about your next year's tax. Little things like tracking your mileage, saving all your receipts, and keeping a log of whom you met and when can translate into hundreds, if not thousands of dollars in your pocket. Virtually everything you do in your life can relate in some way toward furthering your career.

And here's the best news: the government wants you to do this. Yes, they passed a law saying it's legal to take legitimate deductions. So why not take advantage of this? Large corporations and wealthy individuals are doing it.

Taking legitimate deductions does not mean cheating on your taxes. What we are advocating is to take every legitimate deduction that you are entitled to by law. You are in the entertainment business. That means your whole life is directed toward making music your career. Ergo, many situations qualify for a tax deduction as a legitimate expense.

That lunch you had to discuss your music? Deductible. If you're an artist or performer and you are visually in front of the public you can deduct a portion of money for any costumes or hairstyling or drycleaning. CDs; subscriptions to various magazines; transportation to and from gigs; any equipment you purchase—all of it is legitimately deductible if you are planning on running your business as a business.

Yes, some of these deductions may raise a red flag with our country's beloved Internal Revenue Service. You may be one of the rare individuals who are audited. Don't panic. If you have all your receipts and can make a legitimate case that these expenses were used to further your business career, you'll be fine. Remember, when you send in your tax sheet, what you're doing is making a first offer on your eventual settlement for that year with the government. They may decide to dispute your offer and you may have to wrestle to arrive at the final figure. But as long as you have legitimate business purposes for what you claim, you will be fine.

Without a business angle, there would not be a music industry. Jason Howell, a well-known music industry accountant from Washington, D.C., once said at a DIY Convention that an audit is like an impeachment or a court martial; they sound really bad but all they are is official people coming to see what you've done. If you're been doing everything right, you really don't have anything to worry about.

From this point forward, you'll undoubtedly take every deduction you can. But consider—have you taken every deduction you can take from your PAST taxes?

There is an IRS form 1040X that will allow you to go back three years and say, "You know what? I forgot to take some legitimate deductions on my tax forms." And you can go back and make your case, and, in most instances, get some additional money back.

Yes, you are red-flagging yourself just a tad. But red flags do not matter if you are in the right.

There's also an old saw among musicians that you can only claim losses for a certain number of years. But you have every right to claim even more if your motive is to make a profit. Hopefully, you will eventually make a profit and give back to your beloved Uncle Sam as part of the Great American Economy.

In short: don't be afraid to argue the point.

Although the world is moving increasingly toward digital distribution, it's a safe bet that compact discs will remain a part of the music scene for at least the next five years. Thus, creating one that best represents your message is one of the biggest decisions you'll make when starting your business.

Imagine ten CDs lying on a desk in front of you, all of them from artists that you haven't heard of before. You have to choose one of them. What will determine which one you'll bother to open? Clearly, the visual presentation on the front cover will, in most cases, be the determining factor. Interesting artwork wins every time, particularly in a world overrun with mediocre CDs.

Most of the people you will be trying to reach at every level of the music industry, from club bookers to journalists to music supervisors, publishers and labels, have piles and piles of CDs crossing their desk. Since their attention span to any one package is limited, you have to seize the moment and give them an incentive to examine your CD more closely. Such intrigue is the stuff of million-dollar marketing studies in virtually every business that requires an item to sit on the shelf, from corn flakes to compact discs.

Although it's important to have a striking image, it's also important to have an image that fits with your music. A skull and crossbones isn't appropriate for an album of harp music. A paisley flower scene isn't the greatest representation of a non-psychedelic band. And a blurry, brick wall leaning image of a band that doesn't have visual appeal won't do anything to move the CD.

Spend some money on an artist and photographer if no one in the band has that particular talent. Get at least three samples made of a cover design and field-test it among your friends. Next to creating great music, this is the most important decision you'll make. Don't blow it by settling for something that doesn't make an immediate impact on the thousands of people who will see your CD and won't have a clue about the music.

When considering your manufacturing needs, it's also wise to keep enough money in the budget for a jewel box container for your

CD. Although cardboard and transparent sleeves save money, they are generally loathed by anyone who comes in contact with them. Particularly among busy professionals who receive tons of submissions, the cardboard/transparent sleeves tend to get lost in the constant stack of jewel boxed CDs.

Although some progressive people prefer getting links to your MP3 files via e-mail, they remain a distinct minority at this stage of the Net's development.

If you're in a position to ask your potential colleagues which they'd prefer, do so before sending any links. Like cardboard sleeves, sending links without approval sends a subliminal message that mentally devalues the submission. Use with caution.

A key determination if you're having your CDs produced by a manufacturing house is turnaround time. Some unscrupulous dealers take in more work than they can handle and prioritize the manufacturing according to the size of the order. A smaller order is far down the food chain. Some have to broker the work through several vendors, again resulting in a longer turnaround time. Ask around among your friends who have gone through the process.

Also make sure you are getting glass-mastered replicated CDs rather than duplicated CDs, which can lose some integrity in the manufacturing process.

HOW NOT TO RUIN YOUR MUSIC CAREER

1. Set up a business entity that controls your business affairs.
2. Get an agreement among any partners specifying duties.
3. Make sure you can prove you own your work.

7
LICENSING YOUR MUSIC
FOR FILM/TV

Everyone wants to place their music in film and television, and never more so than now, at a time when the traditional record industry is imploding and musicians are looking for varied ways to generate revenue from their compositions.

There are tons of film, TV, video games, commercials and other productions going on around the world that need music. The key to making money is to find out who they are and what they need, then getting your music to them in a timely fashion.

There are several good points to be made for getting exposure via this route. For one, since commercial radio plays little new music, it's an avenue of reaching a large audience that just may be interested in your music if only they could hear some of it.

It's also a way to make money and gain exposure to a pool of other music supervisors and create a buzz about your act and your music. And, of course, it's a way to make money, as your music will generate revenue from its licensing and performances in various media.

Wilson Young is a music supervisor who worked for four seasons on MTV's *The Real World* and also found music for *Road Rules*, *Starting Over* and others.

"We use a lot of music on those shows," said Wilson. "There are probably thirty, forty cues per episode. We do twenty-five episodes a season, so that's two hundred, three hundred cues."

The music supervisors for films, TV and other productions function much in the way that A&R people do at record companies. They deal with various representatives of music acts, go out and hear live shows, do research on the Internet and through magazines, and listen to CDs and MP3s.

They're looking for something that fits the mood of the show or a particular scene. They're also, in most cases, looking for something cost-effective that falls within the show's budget. And they're trying to build a reputation for finding the music that will make their bosses, the show's/film's/game's directors and producers, happy.

Yes, it can sometimes be difficult to reach the right people as a struggling unknown. Almost every entity in the established music industry has people whose job it is to contact music supervisors and allied people who need music. There's a lot of horse-trading and favors that are done in exchange for such consideration. And money often talks.

But in the end, access is all about relationships, relationships, and did we mention relationships?

More and more productions are starting to use music libraries and young unknowns to fill their music needs. The reasons are twofold: young unknowns and libraries often cost less, and the hassle of dealing with them—presuming the young unknowns and libraries have followed the letter of copyright law—can be a lot less trouble than going to a giant  publisher and asking for the rights to put the Beatles in your next film, an action thriller which features a giant orgy between killer squid.

> More and more productions are starting to use music libraries and young unknowns to fill their music needs.

How do you find these fine folks of music supervision? There are many avenues, not the least of which are personal contacts from people who actually work on productions. Regular reading of such trade publications as *The Hollywood Reporter, Variety,* and *AdWeek,* which typically list films, TV shows and commercials in production, is a good way to stay on top of upcoming opportunities.

There are music business directories, such as *The Hollywood Music Industry Directory,* which list music supervisors for film and TV. There are also companies that specialize in placing film and TV music. Most music publishers and record labels also stay in the game.

Two popular Internet sites are also worthy of consideration. LukeHits.com is run by Luke Eddins and is targeted at independent acts. Eddins has a policy of listening to everything that comes in and will not take a fee unless he places your music in a production.

A company called TuneData is also popular among independents and those who seek to place music in productions. The site will, for a fee, e-mail you when a new listing for a production looking for music comes up.

If you're determined to DIY your way to music supervisors, the basic rules of business etiquette apply. Be professional with your submission, be polite in your inquiries, and be persistent in following up.

Most music supervisors get hundreds of submissions and even more phone calls. Getting them to take notice of your precious CD requires the same amount of thought and packaging that you would use to send anyone your work. In other words, send a CD in a plastic bag and it triggers a response that's akin to stepping in a fresh pile of manure.

"I find it very ineffective to just solicit blindly," said Michael Todd, an ASCAP Director of Music & TV. "You have to do some homework and target who you're sending stuff to. Otherwise, it's a waste of money and time. For every 500 CDs you mail out, you may get one call back. You've got to have some way of connecting and separating yourself. And for the most part, people don't take unsolicited material. They just don't. It's a liability for them."

That said, you can make a connection with someone very simply. Some music supervisors will respond to an unsolicited package if it's something they need at the particular moment it arrives in their office, or if they have met the person who has sent it. Many artists send their own CDs out to people they've connected with informally. If you've met a supervisor at a networking event, send them a CD and politely follow-up.

You can also approach existing music libraries and solicit your work for representation. Many of them will take material in return for a cut of the publishing or some other consideration. Be careful, though, on the terms they require. Consult your entertainment attorney before assigning any rights in your compositions.

When you mail your package, your CD should not be a rough demo. "In today's world, you really don't have an excuse when you're comparing yourself to the other people that you're competing against," said Todd, noting the quality of home recording equipment has risen exponentially in the last few years.

Yes, artwork often does count. It creates an impression of your work even before the CD is slipped out of the jacket and into the machine. You are creating an overall work of art. Every impression is precious.

As with A&R people at record labels, the music supervisors have mountains of music to go through. As such, don't put 15 songs on a CD and expect them to find the gem. Two to four tracks, maximum, is plenty for your genius to come shining through. If you have a completed CD with 15 tracks that you'd like to place, highlight a few tracks on the outside of the package when submitting.

A small tip: it is advised that you don't shrink-wrap the CD you send a music supervisor. Many supervisors listen to music in the car on the way to a gig. Getting them unwrapped is a major hassle, as anyone who has struggled with plastic wrapping will attest.

Let's presume for the moment that you've done your homework and found a production that you wish to submit music to for consideration. The best package is the simple one. A CD, a cover letter with some credentials, and that's it. No photos, no files, no press kits. You're trying to sell them one precious song, maybe more. They don't need to know that your mom wouldn't let you ride the pony when you were ten.

One common screw-up that drives music supervisors crazy is a lack of contact information. Make sure everything you send has your full name, your phone and your e-mail. Put your name and contact information directly on the disc and on the jewel box and all the ancillary material you send. Don't make these extremely busy people take time to search for that information. It's just too easy for them to say "pass" and move on to the next project.

Getting your music in a film, TV or video game is a separate issue from getting your song on a film's soundtrack album. Quite often, songs that are featured in films or TV don't make the "official" soundtrack album. There is a tremendous amount of politicking that goes into the selection of tracks for most soundtrack albums, with major labels throwing around money and other fun stuff in order to squeeze a few more acts onto the disc.

Some record labels just give the music away to various productions in hope that the exposure will fuel sales of the recording. The rationale is that the songwriters and publishers will earn money via performance royalties generated by the airing of the show or film, and such exposure will hopefully lead to bigger things for the act. Since many shows and films put links to the music on their web sites, viola—new fans are born.

How much money can you make from licensing? Like Bob Dole answered when they asked him the boxers or briefs question, depends.

The rates vary for each segment of the business. For example, cable television rights pay less than broadcast TV. The money can be anywhere from a few hundred dollars to a few thousand for a song that hits network television. The amount of the check depends on how the song fits in the production, how big a budget the production has, and how badly they want that particular song.

A song that's part of a show can also trigger something called a "favored nations" clause, which means that you'll make as much money as everyone else whose music is being used gets paid. Of course, if your song is used differently than anything else in the film or TV show—for example, if it's the highlight of a key production number in the middle of the show—then you will typically be paid more than music running in the background.

There are two licenses for every song, the sync and the master. The sync is short for synchronization, and it's basically saying you have the right to synchronize the music to a moving image. A synchronization license is the songwriting license, meaning that no matter who has covered that song it's going to be the same sync, even for the different versions. For example, you have the song *My Way*, which was performed by Frank Sinatra and Sid Vicious. That will be the same synchronization license, even though there are two versions of the song.

The master use license is for a particular recording of the song. If you did not write the song, you are not going to have the rights to license the sync. And if you have assigned your rights to a record label that owns an interest in your master recordings, they will have to clear their portion of the deal.

Music can also be licensed in various ways for films that will affect your ultimate compensation. A small indie film may seek a license that includes only the right to use the music in a specific festival.

Many such festival licenses have what are known as "step deals." These aren't deals that are left home scrubbing floors while their mean step-sister deals go to the ball. A step deal is where a caveat is included in the agreement that will allow a film that is in a festival to also be licensed by other festivals and for possible distribution, with differing levels of compensation attached. That way, if a film suddenly gains momentum with audiences and starts generating demand for screenings, the music rights holders who provided the music will be properly compensated.

Mara Schwartz is the director of film, TV and new media for Bug Music, a publishing administrator with offices in Nashville, New York, Los Angeles and London that handles the publishing for over 10,000 accounts. The company has had a hand in such hits as *The Real Slim Shady* by Eminem and *Wide Open Spaces* by the Dixie Chicks, among many others.

Schwartz spends a good chunk of her working day on the phone with music supervisors for film, television, video games, commercials, and other interests. Her mission is to find out what they need and pitch Bug Music clients as possible solutions.

Bug reaches out to the supervisors in several ways. When they have an artist with a new CD, they will make sure to service it to the music supervisors. They also put together compilation discs that can highlight the careers of their clients, a kind of retrospective that underlines the breadth of their work.

"There's also a situation where they will come to us saying that they have a specific cue that needs to be filled, and what do we have in our catalog?" said Schwartz. "Most of the conversations are about what you're working on now and what kind of music they're looking for. We make sure that they at least have an opportunity to hear everything that we have that's appropriate for what they're trying to fill."

Most often, Schwartz says, music supervisors are looking to replace a song that they've already included in their project but can't obtain clearance on.

"Those tend to be very hard to fill," said Schwartz, "because they've already used a certain song, they've fallen in love with that song, and what they really want is that song."

Alas, either the price isn't right or some other quirk of the moment makes the song unattainable by that particular production.

Music supervisors then try to find a substitute. Usually, if they're trying to replace a song by Fat Boy Slim, they'll ask for something that sounds like that. At times, the request can be vague, asking for modern rock or modern dance tracks.

"We've had requests as specific as pre-1934 Turkish music," said Schwartz. "We had some actually. It was for HBO's *Carnivale*. They use authentic music in that show."

The need for music runs year-round, particularly as more and more cable and broadcast networks introduce new programming year-round.

While Schwartz only pitches Bug Music clients, she does have a few hints that can make it easier for the music supervisors to say "yes" to your work.

Owning your own master and publishing rights is one way. A song can be easily cleared with one phone call, a blessing in a business when trying to reach businesses and individuals who lead the peripatetic life of show business legends.

"For me, I think it helps for the songwriters to give me a one-sentence description of each song—what it sounds like and what the topic is—so I can just go through and refer to it really quickly when there are needs that I have. I don't have to sit and listen to every song."

There are hundreds of people on any given day reaching out to plug particular music. Every record label, including most of the smaller ones, assigns someone to make the calls. All of the music publishers also designate people. There are companies that are set up specifically to pitch to film and TV. And a lot of individual artists and/or their managers are working the phones.

Occasionally, they strike gold. Major commercials can pay a few hundred thousand dollars for the rights to use a song.

Another specific problem that can hurt the opportunities available to people who want to get their songs in film and television: you can't use too many specifics or nobody's going to license it.

"A song that goes, "Oh, Suzy, I love you so much," that's not going to get licensed for anything," said Schwartz. "Unless your character is named Suzy, it's just not going to apply. Songs that are positive and have a very general message, "Life is great" or "I love you so much" tend to get licensed more than songs that are bummers. Songs that are super-duper specific, like, "I was riding down Route 1 in my Mercedes listening to George Jones on the stereo" isn't going to get licensed as much as "I'm feeling good and whatever."

Another must for would-be licensees: always have an instrumental version of your song available.

"We have a client, they make beautiful music, and their lyrics are just really depressing," said Schwartz. "I keep saying to them, you know, you're making really good art, and for your album, this is great, but for film and TV licensing, it's terrible."

Everyone should have an instrumental version of all his or her vocal songs, because you never know when you're going to need it.

And when they need it, they'll need it right away. A lot of times there'll be a situation where the vocal is on and then characters start talking and they'll want to switch to an instrumental version in the background. Or where it's a commercial and they'll want to insert a tag line in the middle with an instrumental version. And you should always have both versions because they never realize they want it until they're in the editing room, and we've actually had situations where we've lost placements because the client couldn't get us an instrumental version fast enough. And it's easy to do it when you're in the studio; just lay it down."

One final thought: if you're a vegan and absolutely can't stand the thought of your music supporting a McDonald's commercial, tell the person pitching your music up front.

"If they pitch you for something and you turn it down, they're never going to want to use you again," said Schwartz. "So it's better to not get in that situation in the first place."

Schwartz can't imagine anything unpitchable. "Some of our clients have songs with a lot of bad words in them, but there's a use for them. Sometimes they specifically need bad word songs."

Maybe even songs like yours.

Sampling is part of the culture, and many music supervisors are scared of their use. A sample can either be a part of a recording, where you take a little clip from an existing recording, or you can sample simply by singing or performing a very short part of an existing melody or a lyric. All of it has to be cleared, i.e., approved by the copyright holder, songwriter, and other rights holders.

The first problem is getting the rights to some songs that have 15 writers, as many hip-hop and electronic music samples do.

"Samples are a major problem," said Tyler Bacon, who runs Los Angeles-based Position Music and helps place music in various productions.

"I'm highly paranoid about it. I do a lot of hip-hop and electronic, and those are sample-intensive genres. Artists think that they can sometimes get away with using samples, believing that no one is going to recognize it. And it's amazing how someone somewhere is going to recognize that, and how liable I am if I license that track on your behalf. Even if you went through the proper steps of clearing that license for your record, it doesn't mean it is cleared for licensing that song for a film, because that is a separate right that the copyright holder retains. Most artists don't realize that and think that if it's been cleared for one thing, it's cleared for all. My greatest nightmare is getting that call from Disney or Warner Brothers where a copyright holder heard their sample in a song that I licensed."

To avoid such nightmares, many filmmakers hire a clearance person who deals exclusively with copyright issues. These people seek out the copyright holders and get permission to use various works.

The "temp track" and "temp score" are used by filmmakers and supervisors to get an idea of what kind of music fits with the visual image they're producing. Temp scores are also used for screenings to see how people are reacting to certain sounds.

Directors typically have a dream, an ideal picture of what songs they want in a film. But when it comes time to license the actual music, the director can find out that Led Zeppelin actually wants a lot of money to give up *Black Dog* for the film. That's when it's on to Plan B, which means searching for music from an artist that is less well-known, less expensive, but has the same feel and the same tempo as *Black Dog*.

Increasingly, large music publishers are demanding larger fees for well-known pieces of music. They know if a major director has his or her heart set on a particular song, the movie studio will often acquiesce and provide the funding to obtain it.

Plus, the major music publishers are often owned by multinational corporations that own record companies and need to make up the shortfall from unit sales in some fashion.

In the music supervision world, dealing with such situations is increasingly part of the daily job. Some supervisors and placement experts estimate that half their conversations are about replacement tracks for particular film and TV projects that have hit a stumbling block in their attempts to license a popular track. "I have U2 temped into this show and I need to replace it with something that sounds like it," is a typical exchange.

Knowing that gives an independent artist struggling to place his or her own music an advantage. Do not be afraid to mention on your submission that your music sounds like U2. In an extremely busy segment of the business, it could be the key to licensing your track.

It almost goes without saying (but we'll say it anyway) that if you're sending your music in for consideration for a TV show, you should watch the show and get to know what it's about before you send in your music.

If you have a great song and its feel has nothing to do with the show, it's a waste of everyone's time. *Will & Grace* has little need for death metal.

One tactic gaining popularity is creating your own music library for licensing. For example, a filmmaker might want some instrumental music with a Cajun theme to fit a particular scene. If you have a library of recorded music with that feel (a library can consist of anything from a handful of songs to hundreds) and happen upon a music supervisor in desperate need at the right time, you could score a profitable gig.

Rising in popularity for composers is the art of writing music for video games. Because video games lack a time element, composing for them is especially tricky.

Chris Vrenna is a composer/producer, a member of Nine Inch Nails and has composed for many video games, including the new version of *Doom* released in 2005.

"When you're doing TV or film, you've got the scenes that are edited and you have to score with specific cuts and specific pacing and time," he said. "The problem with games is, you go into a level and a gamer could take ten minutes to two hours to get through that level. So music can't really be written to the picture. You just have to write stuff that really helps create the mood that the game's going for. And the challenge is to make it interesting enough so that kids don't want to turn it off. In films, you don't have an "options" screen to go shut the score off if you're sick of John Williams. It's hard because you're not writing a song."

Writing for video takes a lot longer than doing a film score. One reason is that games are typically tweaked right up to the time they go into production. While a typical film score can take a few weeks to compose, a video game may take a few months.

PJ Bloom is a music supervisor who has worked on soundtracks for Arista and Columbia Records and now runs Neophonic, a Los Angeles-based company.

"We design and execute the musical architecture of any project in which we're involved," said Bloom, explaining his daily work. "And that spans everything from the creative work to budgeting to technical stuff, production work, recording, legal aspects, business affairs, negotiating. It really runs the gamut of business in general."

There are many types of music supervisors, Bloom notes. There are people who deal mostly with songs and others who concentrate on the score. Some go about their duties mechanically, offering whole songs; others try to work to shape the music to the mood of the production.

"For me, the most exciting projects are those where the producers and directors or the studio really have no idea of the musical direction they want to take," Bloom said. "So then I can have as much influence as possible to convince people to go with my ideas. It's generally pretty even. Sometimes, for a particular moment, a director may have a very specific idea about what they want to do and other times they may not know, so I will make a series of suggestions that elicit different emotions and make the picture do different things."

Bloom deals with a range of people involved in the creating of a project, including the director, the producer, the executive producers, and film and TV studio executives.

"I feel like we're kind of unsung in that way, because people don't really realize how completely on the front line we are," Bloom said. "When you're dealing in the creative, the only way to really execute properly is to deal directly with the people who are involved in making those creative decisions."

Bloom has many questions when music is requested, following a process to narrow down the particular type of music for a segment.

"Let's talk about tempo. Are you looking for something that has a lot of energy and that's upbeat? Or are you trying to have something drag on and be a lower-tempo thing? Is it a happy thing? Is it a sad thing? Which character are you playing to? Or are you playing to a general emotion about the film itself. Are you trying to relate some kind of message? Are lyrics important? Do you want the song to speak specifically to the action that's happening? Are you trying to foreshadow something? Are you trying to hark back to something? Those creative questions tend to help me lock in a little bit more definitively what we're trying to do."

Once the preliminary determination is made, Bloom begins the task of locating the proper tracks. His company maintains a huge CD collection that is sorted into various time periods and genres. "And I tend to keep specific libraries within reach for the projects that I'm working on," he said. "I personally have an unhealthy knowledge of music from the last 200 years, which is not necessarily a prerequisite for a music supervisor. That just happens to be because I'm a huge fan in general and just feed off that kind of knowledge."

Bloom estimates that he licenses between $3 million to $5 million worth of music per year. "And that's dispersed everywhere, from major labels and publishers to the most indie of indie person you can think of."

There's no secret to reaching Bloom and people like him.

"There is not one definitive guide that says which music supervisors are working on what projects at any specific moment," he said. "But there is an incredible amount of resource material out there if you look for it. There's the Film & Television Music Guide that I like quite a bit, because it has everybody at most record companies and publishing companies, music supervisors, music editors, agents, composers and a pretty good list. I also tell people you can look in the trade papers a couple times a week. They have the listings for television productions, and current film productions. It won't generally say who the music supervisor is, but you can probably get a good idea about a particular project. At least get a title of something that's in production that you may be interested in, then go on the Internet and try to find out about this film. If it's an action movie, you can use deductive reasoning and figure that they're probably going to want one kind of music. If it's a love story, they're probably going to want another kind of music. The information is out there but it's not going to be handed to anybody on a silver platter."

If you want to reach Bloom, keep it brief.

"You can feel free to call me, but we're always so busy here and the general rule for music supervisors who work at this level is you just need to make your conversations as brief as possible and show respect. I think a common mistake that people make when they call music supervisors is they just say, "Hey, what are you working on?" And that is really, really frustrating, because the bottom line is you don't really want to know what I'm working on. You just want to know how you can get involved in whatever that is."

Bloom suggests that would-be indies cut to the core of any conversation.

"You can call up and say: this is who I am, this is what I have, are you looking for anything like that? And then that conversation will evolve naturally. I wouldn't want to, nor do I have the time to tell you everything that I'm working on."

For those looking to break into music supervision, Bloom advises working with someone already in the field.

"I was involved with established music supervisors and I also got involved with friends or acquaintances who were making independent films and just said, "Hey, let me do this thing for you. You don't have to pay me. I'll figure it out and learn as I go. And ultimately, I just managed to figure out a way to make a living doing it. It's a very,

very difficult field to start from scratch. There are not a lot of us that do it and even fewer that do it successfully. But I highly recommend it. It's incredibly gratifying and you really get to touch so many corners of this business."

HOW NOT TO RUIN YOUR MUSIC CAREER

1. Develop relationships with supervisors and be brief in your contacts.

2. Target appropriate programming for your music.

3. Understand that samples and multiple rights holders make clearances difficult, reducing your changes for placement.

8
MUSIC PUBLISHING

Music publishing is one of the murkiest worlds in the music industry, filled with terminology that makes the average person's head swim. But it's a part of the music world that everyone needs to pay close attention to, because it's one of the few areas where the money flows despite the number of units sold.

First and foremost, learn the first rule of the music business: DO NOT SELL YOUR PUBLISHING. We repeat, DO NOT SELL YOUR PUBLISHING.

Inducing such sale is a common scam in the business. A manager, a record label, an agent, a producer, attorney, accountant or other middlemen demand a share of your publishing rights in return for services rendered or about to be rendered. Why do they do that? Because they know that it's one of the most valuable assets you will create and has the least encumbrances of anything attached to music.

Look back at the history of rock 'n roll and you'll see some sad tales. Morris Levy, who ran Roulette Records and later was convicted of two counts of extortion in connection with a music industry scandal in the 1980s, managed to attach his name to several big hits, including *Heartbreak Hotel*. Levy couldn't carry a tune in a bucket. But he did know that the revenue from music publishing far outlasts that of the recording and can generate money by different artists and in different media from now until the end of time.

What does a music publisher do? When you're a songwriter, the minute you create a song, you have certain rights. And what a music publisher does is handle those rights. You're entitled to certain amounts of money for the exploitation of your composition. A music publisher collects this money and exploits the copyright throughout the world to earn more money.

Starting a publishing company is relatively simple. You declare, "I'm a music publisher," and poof! There you go.

A publisher can also hook you up with other writers and advise in other ways. They can provide some marketing funds. Many people look at music publishers as a bank, because they function in that way. You've already created your work. Now it's up to them to get the most mileage out of it.

Which publisher should you choose? A larger publisher may be able to offer a larger advance and has much more leverage than a smaller publisher. But they also have many more clients to deal with. The personal touch and larger dollop of attention that a smaller publisher can offer may well offset the money.

Be advised, though, that in return for the money, the publishing company takes over the co-rights to the composition, much as a record company owns the masters.

There's a third route to consider in music publishing. Starting a publishing company is relatively simple. You declare, "I'm a music publisher," and poof! There you go. You can take that right to a copyright administration company (Bug Music is one example of the many out there), wherein the business of exploiting your copyright is done for you in return for a percentage of the income. They do everything a major publisher does except for the advance.

There are four major sources of publishing income:

I.   Print income — which includes when a publisher licenses your music for use in any sort of sheet music or folio.

2. Synchronization — which is when someone wants to use your music in connection with a film, television, or any audio/visual medium.
3. Public performance royalties — which entitles you to money for public performances of your music.
4. Mechanical income — which record labels pay to you as a publisher for use on an album.

A publisher is like a stock analyst, trying to determine the potential of an act's music in relation to the investment that will be required to attain the product.

In the old days, when performers and songwriters were in distinct camps, the publishers played a larger role, dishing out the repertoire to singers. But as music evolved and more and more singer/songwriters began to develop their own material, the publishers receded into the background. Today, they still play that role in certain segments of popular music—they are particularly strong in the country and pop markets—but have evolved into a solid, steady source of income in a world beset by all sorts of distractions and downturns to revenue streams. In the case of publishing, it doesn't matter if you bought a video game instead of a CD—they will still derive revenue from licensing the music to the game, whereas the record company may have lost out on a unit sale because a kid spent his $20 on the game instead of the CD.

You can be signed to two different publishers, although it is not common. Some artists are signed to different publishers for different portions of their catalog, or may have a single song placed with one publisher. In general, you're an exclusive writer for a designated term if you sign with a publisher.

Determining who is a songwriter on a composition is a big area for discussion. Under copyright law, as soon as two people get together to write a composition and they contribute music, there's an equal share in the composition. It doesn't matter if you're the drummer or the bass player and you write part of the song and other people make up the rest. The split is still equal unless there's a written agreement that stipulates otherwise.

If you're like most bands starting out, a lot of creative time is spent together in the rehearsal room, which all are sharing and paying for equally. It's an all-for-one, one-for-all atmosphere.

Then a little success is poured into the mixture, and things can change. So it's important to have that partnership agreement in place. And if you're the drummer or bass player, learn to write it!

There's no set number of songs you should have written before approaching a publisher. You could have written a quarter of a song on a hip-hop record that hits No. 1 on the charts, garnering you a cool $100,000. You could have written 3,000 songs and all of them are garbage. Like the recorded side of the business, the publisher is going to look at all the factors that go into the making of an act—who is backing them, their track record and momentum, their style in relationship to what's popular—and then make a determination. They'll listen to the first eight notes of your demo and determine that you're a songwriter worth backing. So don't worry about having a truckload of material.

There are a number of things you can do on your own to get placement. You can get your music in a student film or grassroots compilation, have someone else cover it, or get some action happening in the TV/game world. All of the activity builds momentum, gives you a story, and will help your leverage in determining if you eventually sign with a publisher or administrator.

One way to shop your material is through the online music companies. SongLink.net is one particular opportunity. The company will, for a $250 yearly fee, send out a monthly listing of music opportunities for placement of your music. The company also has a bead on the non-U.S. market, a great way to stay in touch with a revenue stream that's particularly hefty.

Michael Eames is the president of PEN Music Group, which handles the Bob Marley catalog for the U.S. and Canada, among other things. He spends his day balancing a mix of administrative and creative decisions.

"You've got to make sure the songs are registered with ASCAP or BMI or the Copyright Office. You've got to make sure that any records that are out there have licenses and they're paying you proper royalties. You've got to make sure that anything that's used in film and television has a proper license. Are you getting paid? Anything that just pertains to agreements, licenses, rights and royalties is the administrative side, and we have to deal with that every day."

Attached to that array of music, Eames and his staff field daily requests from people who wish to use the music under his company's control.

"So we have to field those requests, get information on what the use entails, go back to the writers and artists for approval, and negotiate the terms and issue the license, essentially, seeking out any opportunity that is out there," he said.

In theory, such activity is not much different from a record company. "They have staff that is theoretically supposed to be dealing with all this," said Eames. "But like any company these days, those responsibilities are being spread out among fewer staffers. We either are working completely separately or in tandem, or the publisher might work completely alone."

Getting on board with an independent publisher like Eames is usually a matter of finding out if they are open to submissions.

"If we are, it's all in the representation. If we were to get two CDs, one of which is something that was burned at home with handwriting on the insert to the CD and another one which was a full-blown CD with great artwork that looks like one that I could go out and buy in the store, we're going to go to the one with the artwork first to listen to it. It just looks as if this person has taken care in what they're doing and is sensitive to how they're presenting themselves to the world. And that image, that look, that presentation, and can many times speak directly to what the music is about, what they are about as an artist or band."

Most independent publishers are more open to receiving unsolicited material than the larger, more corporate publishers.

"Especially in the world of licensing," says Eames, "the downsizing of the corporate part of the music business has unleashed a whole bunch of people from either the publishing side or the record side.

They've lost their jobs and some of them are popping up and saying, "Hi, I'm starting a licensing company." And so there are probably more opportunities now than ever before for an independent DIY artist to search out and find someone who would like to champion what they're doing and make the effort to go out and try to generate some money than there were two or three years ago."

Traditionally, the independent publisher's selling point has been attention rather than a huge advance on publishing rights. "We will jump in the trenches and we don't have near as many artists that we have to make happy like the bigger guys do," said Eames. "You're important, you're the focus, you can get us on the phone."

Unfortunately, the impact of so many new companies chasing the same licensing opportunities has generally driven down the fees for independent artists. The newer companies are accepting lower licensing fees in order to gain a track record, feeling that the artist will still receive revenue from performing rights.

"It's really starting to force all of us, if we want to stay in the game, to accept lesser fees," said Eames. "Money has been generally going down from what was available years ago in a music licensing budget."

Still, Eames said, new artists who are more savvy about retaining rights to their masters are crafting better deals from publishers and record companies.

"It's really becoming more of a partnership in revenue sharing," said Eames. "Someone who knows their business, knows their audience and has worked at it is probably in a stronger position than they've ever been in determining what their future could be."

HOW NOT TO RUIN YOUR MUSIC CAREER

1. Don't sell your publishing!
2. Have your partnership agreement in place before songwriting.
3. Register your songs with the copyright office.

9
PUBLICITY, MARKETING, AND PROMOTION

The best thing about publicity is that it's a free ad.

The worst thing about publicity is that it can be a free ad that slams your band. And there's pretty much nothing you can do about it, unfair or not.

It's time to consider one of the prime movers in gathering attention: the power of the press.

There are hundreds of newspapers, magazines, 'zines, online sites, and blogs that cover music. There are also a few radio and TV shows that feature some local music. The key is reaching them at a time when they're receptive to your music and then selling them on the notion that you are the person they'd like to feature.

There are many types of press you can chase. But for beginning bands, the most realistic is a review.

A review asks someone to either: a) listen to your CD; or b) come down and see you at your next live gig.

Which is easier to obtain? It depends on the media outlet, the critic, the time of day, the amount of things on their desk, whether the publicist is friends with them, if the person likes to go out to shows, if you're playing at 11 p.m. on a Sunday or 8 p.m. on a

Tuesday, if your publicist is a hottie, if you're not in conflict with the World Series... you get the picture.

The biggest determining factor, though, on whether you'll even get a review is the size of the audience wielded by the media outlet in question.

Typically, the larger the publication, the less daring they are in their choices of what to review. No matter how much lip service they pay to the concept of giving everyone a fair shot, it's highly unlikely that the New York Times will review an obscure local act unless it's part of a larger trend or scene.

The good news is that there are plenty of places that are eager to come check you out, no matter your size or status. Local 'zines and online outlets are the heart and soul of independent music. And a lot of them are used as tip sheets by the larger media (not to mention record labels, radio and others looking to pick up on an early buzz). Some 'zines—the online site Pitchfork, for example— have an audience that's nearly at mass media heights and mean more to the audience you're trying to reach than any print publication.

Beyond print, radio is also a source of instant free publicity. Talk radio needs a constant churn of guests. The key is defining your area of expertise and being available when you are needed.

In the early stages of your career, you can pretty much do your publicity by yourself. The best way to reach the outlets you want to reach is by finding out who at those outlets you want to review your music. Nothing goes over like a personal invitation or note with your CD.

What should you enclose in your package if you've never been reviewed anywhere? Simple: a note telling the outlet that you've never been reviewed anywhere and that they can be the first to get in on the story. Don't be afraid to offer to buy a drink or hook them up when they arrive. It's not rocket science. Treat the person well who's about to pass critical judgment on your product and they'll likely be kindly disposed toward you.

Once you've gotten a few reviews together, you start to build what's known in the media business as "a story," which means that there seems to be a groundswell of attention on you and your music.

This groundswell often puts you in line for a feature in a larger publication. Maybe you're starting a local scene. Maybe you and a few other bands are starting to attract attention. Maybe your front woman is the wildest thing that's ever been seen in this part of Oregon.

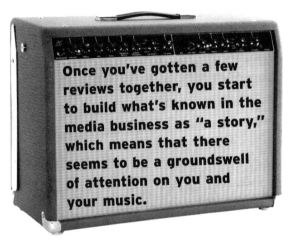

Once you've gotten a few reviews together, you start to build what's known in the media business as "a story," which means that there seems to be a groundswell of attention on you and your music.

Whatever it is that's causing others to write and talk about you, it's a story, and an interesting one to your community.

At some point in your career, hopefully sooner than later, you might reach a stage where you'll be so busy with the other aspects of your career that you've decided to hire someone to spend time contacting media outlets on your behalf. This person may have better relationships and connections with some of the larger media outlets, or may be better at spinning a story on the lowly likes of you than you are capable of creating.

This person is known as a publicist. Their job is to get you mentioned, help get in the ear of the tastemakers, and create a buzz. Some of the more skillful ones know how to play various media outlets against each other, creating a frenzy to tell the story of wonderful you. Others know how to work online, working the proper angles in IMs and chat and board postings to let others know about you.

Still others are merely friendly people who know how to work a room and get the word out to the right people. Sometimes, being associated with the right firm will give your act cache simply by being a client of this uber-publicist. After all, these people are tastemakers, so their perceived taste in clients reflects well on your prospects.

You should be forewarned that no one will guarantee you any coverage. If you're the worst band in the world and have no following to speak of, the best publicist won't be able to generate any real heat.

But if you're on the verge of building something, hiring someone may be one of the best investments you can make. The right press can take an act to the next level and bring out the kind of crowds eager to be in on something that's just about to happen.

Naturally, the cost for hiring someone to do this kind of activity can be expensive. Every publicist has a different price and many will charge you based on what sort of functions you require. Some may even work for free or charge a reduced fee if they believe you're really happening and will bring cache to their own business. But typically, the fees can range from $1000-$3000 a month for a beginning act.

For that amount of money, you can expect the publicity person to devise some innovative ideas on getting your story out there; construct your press kit; contact the media to tout your music and appearances; help coordinate any events, like a record release party, and keep track of where stories on your band appear.

Most new bands will have to do enormous amounts of legwork on their own before even considering a publicist. The simple fact is that most media outlets that consistently cover new bands online and in print can be easily reached without the aid of a publicist.

The mainstream press will typically only jump on your bandwagon when there's a significant story to tell, e.g., you're selling out shows across town, you're getting extensive radio airplay, or you've done something else innovative and newsworthy.

When you've reached that level, you may still wish to handle your own campaign. But know that the publicist does more than place stories—they also have the ear of the media outlets and can plant the right suggestion at the right time. Like many busy professionals, people at newspapers, magazines, online sites and other media outlets are inundated with pitches on new bands, new trends, new CDs. They need a filter, and the publicist is one of the ways they help divide the wheat from the chaff.

There are also do-it-yourself online sites that will bundle your press release with others and send them out en-masse to the press. They charge a fee ranging from $25 to several hundred dollars. While these missives are read by the media, it's akin to sending a note in a bottle via the sea. Lumped in with announcements of all types, the releases blur together in a blend of hype and so what.

Of course, no publicist can guarantee that whomever chooses to write about your music will like it. It's worth noting that no act in the history of entertainment has ever escaped the inevitable bad review. None of that is career killing, but it is a bump in the road, particularly if the critic whose venom you draw is perceived as influential.

That said, a bad review can, in some cases, prove to be a good thing in the long run. If nothing else, it's yet another piece of attention that will draw the curious to your shows and, perhaps, check out your music and see for themselves.

Tracey Miller is a publicist that grew up in the independent record business, running her own label, Fake Doom Records, then segueing into publicity at one of the big independent labels of the 1980s and early 1990s, Profile Records.

Today, Miller runs her own firm and works with such artists as Run-DMC and India Arie, in addition to new independent acts.

Her typical day begins with e-mailing and reviewing previous works, "what I did the day before and what wasn't completed and following up on that," Miller said. "If I spoke to someone and pitched an idea and have to get back to them, I review the notes. I also review my notebooks on each artist or project that I'm working on, and then come up with an idea or a pitch or TV show or somewhere else where I need to be on that artist."

Miller's extensive note taking serves her well as she deals with artists and managers who call in, asking for updates on where they are with certain projects.

With a new artist, "the publicist's job is to create awareness," said Miller. "It's always about a story—what else is going on with that artist at radio and retail. Sometimes you can just build a press story, but it's hard, because there are so many new artists out there. It's a process where you have to start and just keep adding, and did I mention it's hard work?"

Miller advises contacting a publicist "when you've built up a story. It's hard to pay for an independent publicist unless you're going to be creative about the financing and give up a piece of the publishing or record. At the end of the day, we all need to pay for our time, and ultimately, until there's a story and you have some things in place, it's really not cost-effective to have an independent come on board."

Start regionally and grow from there, Miller said. "Ask yourself, what's my goal? What do you want to achieve? And then structure your plan of attack on the media based on that. It doesn't make sense to send your record out to the Smithtown Journal in Oklahoma if you're not going to be performing there."

"Ultimately," Miller says, "my job is to take information and spin it into the best possible story, taking information and repackaging and repositioning and regurgitating."

HOW NOT TO RUIN YOUR MUSIC CAREER

1. Reach out to the appropriate level of media.
2. Build a story.
3. Start regionally rather than nationally.

Marketing is different from promotion and publicity, but often gets lumped into one or both categories. The differences between the categories are subtle, but definitive, and should never be confused.

Promotion is a direct method of touting yourself. It can take the form of advertising, where you buy a billboard, a radio spot or an ad in the local alternative weekly. It can be the simple act of putting up a flier on a telephone poll or making sure your name is on the marquee at the club you're playing. Promotion is a direct way to get the word on your music and your appearances out to a wider audience and usually involves your direct involvement in making it happen.

Publicity is when a nominally objective third party decides to discuss you and/or your music. This is usually done without your direct input, but may be guided by a publicist, and includes reviews, features and commentaries in all manner of media on you and your art. It attempts to paint a picture of where you're at and where you're going, giving context to your place in the universe.

Marketing combines elements of publicity and promotion, but actually is a separate entity that attempts to snare loyalty by subtly manipulating the emotions of potential customers and create an affinity for a product. In this case, that's you or your band. Understanding marketing is as simple as pondering the effect that certain images or sounds have on you. You see a car commercial on television. The person driving the car is surrounded by a good-looking companion in the passenger seat as they zoom along a highway along the coast to the beat of the latest music. You like that ad. You think the person driving the car has their life together, able to afford a hot car, a hot companion, and all the finer things in life that comes with that ability. You want to be the person in the driver's seat.

The ad has created an affinity within you. You feel that by driving that car, you will be cool, desirable to attractive people, perceived as a person of wealth and influence, and able to enter the inner sanctum with a wave of your hand.

That, my friends, is marketing. It's creating an aspiration within you that applies to a person, product or event. You want to be a part of the thing generating that emotion, so you will go out and buy that car or CD, try to go to that restaurant, wear that sweater or sneaker. You want to feel that emotion that comes only with being a part of that experience.

Humans are inevitably pack animals. Despite all the protestations to the contrary, it's extremely rare to find something so original, so unique that it stands apart from everything that has come before. Thus, smart marketers realize that if they can tap into that longing that we have hidden in our core, the love that dares not speak its name, they can win you over to their cause.

Marketing is really the most fun part of the music business, because it's truly the most magical thing in it. When it works, it almost takes on a life of its own, drawing people together who feel that they can bond together because of their affinity for your music.

Think not? Go to a Death Cab for Cutie concert and take a look around at the audience. A large portion will look like record store clerks (because, in fact, many are, but that's beside the point). They come together in celebration of their shared taste.

The same can be said for any number of acts, from teen pop to death metal to classical music. Usually, there's a formula involved that's as old as the first pop star. The idea is to make the girls love you and the boys aspire to be you (please note, whatever your sexual orientation, variations on that theme still hold true. You do the math).

This has been true since the time when people danced around the campfire while Ugg beat on his log. And will be true long into the future, when XHYGH plays on a singing rock in his hot new club on Alpha 4.

How can you create a marketing buzz? The first step is to define whom you want to reach. That means profiling your audience and determining what they have in common.

Now, I hear you wailing already—"but everyone loves our music. You look out in the crowd and see young, old, black, white, Asian, all united in their love for our music. We don't want to pigeonhole ourselves."

It's all in the way you look at your audience. While the way they dress and their outward demographics can provide a clue, there are also other considerations.

Even within a range of ages, race, color, creed, there is usually one aspirational dynamic at play that brings together an audience. It may simply be the need to feel like they're on the cutting edge, more sophisticated, hipper than thou. It may be that everyone in the house attended the same high school and want to support the local act. Or it may be that everyone in the crowd feels that this music represents their inner voice, speaking to their pent-up desire to finally express what they've always wanted to express.

Thus, white kids from the suburbs flock to hip-hop. Young people are fans of Tony Bennett and Tom Jones. Prince has an audience united in its love of creative genius.

One of the ways many businesses help to define where they are at and where they're heading is to have a plan.

A business plan details the specifics of your business, its missions, assets/liabilities, overall strategy and tactics. But a marketing plan is a separate creature. It describes who your customers are and the way you plan to identify and capture them, plus retain them once they are on board.

The marketing plan can be the biggest part of your business, because it focuses on the most important part of your success: the customer, who, in the case of musicians, is known as the fan.

The fan is the core of what you do as a musician. They are the people who gladden the hearts of most of the ancillary businessmen who comprise the music industry. These include the club owner, the concert promoter, the retailer, the radio man, the manager, the attorney, the accountant. All care about the fan. Because without the fan, there is no business. You may still be a great musician, but none of the businesses that are built around supporting music and making money from that support will care, because there's nothing in it for them.

The fan must be nurtured. Selling to the fan is but one aspect of the deal that you concoct with them. The rest of the time is about creating a sense of community, of affinity, of aspiration and enjoyment.

A fan must be encouraged to tell their friends and work hard to bring them into your tribe. They are your sales team in the street.

Be warned, fans can quickly be turned off by bad marketing. If you take a left turn away from your core message to the fans, you may turn them off, or, worse, offend them.

Marketing embraces everything from the artwork on your CD and promotional materials, to merchandising, the way the band looks, the choice of venues you play, even the price of your shows. It is about defining who you are and what you're about for both you and them.

A good marketer knows who her audience is and how to push their buttons. A great marketer knows how to take advantage of the audience once those buttons are pushed and translate them into sales.

A marketing plan has several elements, but there are no carbon copies of plans. They can be long or short, depending on your inspiration. And certainly, they must be constantly revised as circumstances change, both within your career and from outside events.

First, a marketing plan typically assesses your strengths and your weaknesses. Your strengths will detail who you are and what assets are your disposables that will allow you to enact your marketing plan. Your weaknesses will define the barriers to achieving that success.

Brutal honesty is the best policy in writing the marketing plan. It's designed to help you, and sunny assessments of your prospects that are based on hope and faith won't help you take the practical steps that are necessary to achieve your goals.

For example, if you've yet to perform at the top nightclub in town, it doesn't really make sense to write a marketing plan for a stadium tour. Similarly, if you can't afford to take out a gatefold spread in *Rolling Stone*, planning for it is sheer lunacy.

The marketing plan is designed to overcome those barriers by allocating the proper resources.

So, let's say your band's greatest strength is its photogenic appeal. Clearly, you will plan to get a clear image of the group on all of your promotional materials so that the people who will respond to your sex appeal see it.

Along those lines, the next step in a good marketing plan is assessing your opportunities to exploit your strengths and avoid your weaknesses.

If every club specializing in hard rock music in your area has closed recently, it's a good sign that the fickle tide of public taste has gone out on the genre, at least in your area. While that trend can be reversed, it's more than likely a sign that you're not going to be an overnight sensation in your area as a band in that specialty niche.

Part of your marketing plan should be a strategic statement on what you plan to do. Specifics count, so even if your plan is world domination and a stadium tour in two years, it's not very helpful to put that on a piece of paper.

Rather, it's time to focus on the immediate steps you need to take in order to achieve realistic goals within a short-term time frame.

For example, one aspect of your marketing plan can be "We plan on offering the best stage show in Eastern Pennsylvania." Such a statement means you are aware of your competitors and what they're using, and will attempt to make your calling card much better than your competition.

One other aspect of your marketing plan can be, "We will offer major discounts to fans that sign up for our mailing list via our web site." That works if your fan base is highly wired and sets up the site as a primary means of communication.

Once you have your strategy in place, it's time to set down your objectives. This is the place where you will devise ways to measure your progress in achieving what you've set down.

The objectives should be fairly easy to measure: we plan to increase attendance at our live shows by 150 people by the end of August. So, if attendance at your last show in June was X, what was it at the end of August?

Another: We plan to increase our mailing list by 1000 people by the end of the summer. If your web site had Y number of members at the beginning of July, how many did it have at the beginning of September?

The next section of your marketing plan outlines the tactics to achieve that objective. This is the crucial step in the plan, for it puts down the means by which you hope to achieve your objectives. If your goal was to increase your mailing list, it should outline a way to do so, e.g., "We plan to have two model-types at each show snagging people to sign up for the list."

Naturally, some of your tactics will require money. You also should set down how much each of your tactics should cost. The two models at the show may do it for $25 a pop, or it may cost nothing at all if someone's cousin does it. Either way, you set the step in a way that clearly outlines what you plan to do.

Things can happen along the way to alter your strategy and results may disappoint, causing a switch in strategy. Perhaps the cousin you chose to sign people up for the mailing list becomes obnoxious after a few drinks, thus causing low signups. Perhaps the signatures on the document are illegible.

But at least you will have a plan in place and be able to spot the trend. Instead of waiting until the end of the summer to declare your marketing plan a disaster, you can take steps in the interim to mitigate problems.

One of the finer examples of marketing genius at work in popular music is Jimmy Buffet. Here's a singer/songwriter with origins in the neo-folkie scene, where he made little impact. He moves on to a major record label, records one Top 10 hit, *Margaritaville*, and then releases a string of albums that rarely make a ripple in the national charts.

But, lo and behold, Jimmy Buffet is one of the top concert attractions in America, and runs an empire that includes restaurants, books, merchandise and, finally, his own record label. How does he do it?

Jimmy Buffet has tapped into the magic of marketing. He realized that a lot of people who are stuck in humdrum, day-to-day living secretly desire to chuck it all and escape to a land where the sun is shining, the ocean water is warm and the margaritas are cold, where cares melt away and you can relax and enjoy.

Thousands upon thousands of people have a one-day ritual during the summer, when they gather in parking lots and celebrate that longing. Sure, they like Buffet, and celebrate his songs with an almost religious fervor. But what they're really celebrating is a lifestyle. Jimmy Buffet isn't the best singer or songwriter; he certainly isn't a big sex symbol; and he hasn't lived a particularly high-profile life in the media. Yet he has a solid core of fans who identify with the good times that his music conjures; they aspire to that, or at least dream that they do. And they'll keep coming back each year to celebrate that lifestyle, recruiting new friends along the way who may not be into Buffet, but certainly don't mind having a few drinks in a collegial atmosphere.

That's the type of mood you have to create. There's no one path to achieving it, and sometimes calculating that sort of audience can backfire. But it's worth noting that self-awareness on the part of the musician or group can go a long way toward channeling your promotion and publicity in the right direction.

If you know that your audience largely listens to a certain radio station and goes to a particular circle of clubs and reads a type of publication, then you can more easily target your publicity and promotion money at that audience. If you're in a death metal band, for instance, you wouldn't take out a full page ad in *Whole Life Times*, which appeals to the granola set.

No, you take your skull and bones logo and put it in the local paper that caters to your audience.

Defining yourself isn't something to be ashamed of. Derek Sivers, the founder of CDBaby, the online retail store that brought a fresh and honest approach to CD distribution, frequently tells a funny story about musicians and their reluctance to talk about what type of music they make.

"Well, man, it's kind of like, a little of this and that," goes the story as told by Sivers (believe me, it's funnier in person). "You really have to come out and hear it. We're playing this Sunday night."

Imagine if the tables were turned. You meet a businessman and ask him what kind of business he runs.

"Well, man, it's kind of like, we do things," the businessman would say. "We're out on Route 17. You have to stop by and see it."

Would you get in your car and drive out to Route 17 to see the store? Of course not. So why on God's great earth would you suppose that someone, given an equally vague description of your music, will choose to come out and see you on a Sunday night?

Remember, you're building an audience beyond your family and friends, who will come out to see you at least twice. Your object is to create an ever-widening circle of like-minded people who want to become a part of your success story, so that they can tell people they saw you playing at a tiny little place way back before you began playing stadiums.

Kashif is an artist who has been a major record label recording artist and producer for many years, selling about 70 million records, by his own reckoning, each of them going gold (500,000 units sold) or platinum (one million units sold).

Early in 2004, he issued his sixth CD.

"But I will tell you, that as the artist you know as Kashif, I have not made that much money selling my own CDs through the major record label system, even though my records are pretty big," he told the audience at the 2004 DIY Convention. "Most of my money has been made producing."

He continued, "The fact of the matter is, when you are an independent artist, and even when you're not an independent artist, you are an entrepreneur. You have to do the same things that other entrepreneurs and other corporations do."

To pump his sixth CD, Kashif devised an ingenious marketing plan. He instituted a referral service wherein people referred people to his web site to get the new CD. When he reached 25,000 units sold, the person with the most referrals would get their rent or mortgage paid for three months.

"You have to be creative in your approach," said Kashif. "The reason I thought this was such a good idea is because it hits everybody right in the gut. What do we worry about the most? Paying our mortgage, paying our rent, and paying our car notes."

Kashif knows his audience well. He also promoted his latest album by performing in, of all places, a barbershop.

"My music is urban AC, that means black folks mostly buy my music and grown black folks. I'm not saying that white folks don't buy it and I'm not saying that I don't want you all to buy it, but I know my demographic and I know that one thing black folks like to do is have their hair sharp. So we go to go to the barbershop on Friday, because we go to the club on Friday night, and the ladies they go to the salon on Fridays and Saturdays. So I'm going to visit hair salons, where there a whole bunch of black women sitting in there getting their hair done, and sing to them."

Remember that this is a man who has sold 70 million records. And even if he sells ten at a barbershop, everyone he meets there will tell their friends, who will tell their friends, who will tell their friends. Instant awareness. That's marketing.

Thinking outside the box is an over-used term when it comes to marketing, but the most successful campaigns are great examples of doing so.

Steve Levesque, an artist manager who runs Luck Media & Marketing in Los Angeles, used such thinking in a campaign for his brother's band, Agent Orange.

"What we did is we found out that a lot of skateboarders liked the band and so we started playing skateboard parks," said Levesque. Then we got a skateboard deal, and we were in a skateboard video. So when we were on tour, instead of doing an in-store at a record store, we would actually perform at a skateboard shop and have a raffle for a skateboard. And that built a very, very big following with a certain type of consumer."

Finding that kind of consumer is the first job of the new act. The hardest thing for most musicians is being honest about their influences. Hoping to avoid being pigeonholed as a certain type of act, the musician resorts to vague descriptions of their music, hoping that such obfuscation will cause them to be lumped into that indefinable netherworld of acts and therefore distinguish them from the great mass.

Wrong approach. If you don't define yourself, others will do it for you. The first time your band is reviewed, the person reviewing the show will take your indefinable sound and clearly state that you're a cross between Creed, Britney Spears, and Frank Zappa.

So your first task is to define what you sound like. Pick three musicians you admire and that fit with your style and say, it's like Lenny Kravitz meets James Brown, or something along those lines. Hone your elevator pitch, as they say in venture capital circles. That means you should come up with a phrase that can be delivered quickly, as one would do if they met an important executive in an elevator and had three seconds to deliver the pitch.

If you don't define yourself, others will do it for you.

The idea is usually to keep it simple. In television lore, the best pitch ever was for *Miami Vice*, which was described as "MTV Cops." The tactic can actually lead to more interest in your music. Who wouldn't want to go see a band that played "hillbilly flamenco," as one notable act once described itself?

Along with getting a handle on what kind of music you're producing, it's wise to develop an idea of who your audience is and how best to reach them. This is what anyone you hire to do your marketing, promotion and publicity will do. But it pays off to develop that sense at the earliest stages of your act, because these are the people who will form your core audience, the die-hards who were there at the beginning of it all.

Your job is to find that consumer first and then cater to them. They are the people who have to be happy before you can broaden your appeal. If you can't make a small audience happy, you certainly won't be any more successful with a large one.

The name of your band and its logo will go a long way toward establishing your identity. Imagine, if you will, a triple bill of bands that features Judas Priest, Iron Maiden and a third act. What's an appropriate name for this audience, which obviously likes its music hard? What kind of music would you expect that act to play? What kind of logo would you expect them to have? What color t-shirt would their fans wear?

Broadening your perspective, where would these fans hang out in their spare time? What beer would they like to drink? What kind of car would they drive? What would they expect from a show of this type?

You get the picture. By building up presumptions of what your audience wants, you'll unlock a lot of opportunities to build word of mouth and attendance at your shows, make some money on merchandise, and develop a mailing list of hard-core fans.

We'll repeat this several times in the coming chapters of the book, but we'll say it here now for particular emphasis: the most important thing you can do to build your act is to grow your mailing list.

Let's presume for a moment that you have the playing and per-

The most important thing you can do to build your act is to grow your mailing list.

forming thing pretty much down (a big assumption, I know, but bear with us). You might be happy performing for the rest of your life in your living room, but, if you're like most musicians, eventually you're going to want to get out and perform, see people singing your lyrics back to you, meeting girls/boys, drinking, carrying on and generally having a good time in public.

The key to all of that is the e-mail list. Why? Because it's your most direct method of contact with your fans. You can spend time and effort sending out post cards; you can telephone; you can post messages on web sites. But you have a direct, intimate, one-to-one relationship established with anyone who signs up for your e-mail list. Through such a list, you can announce a gig, prep people for a special show, let them know about the progress of your CD, talk about the band and, in general, build a lasting bond. It's your lifeline and every show is an opportunity to get more people aboard.

Many bands have assigned specific people to go about the task of gathering names. It's considered as important as the performance. A word of advice: try and get someone good-looking, outgoing, and with good hygiene to encourage signups. As much as the band is required to be presentable, so is your representative on the floor. Cousin Artie isn't necessarily the best choice for this important task.

New laws that aim to prevent spam have made it important to get opt-in names. Save the signup sheets and use a mailing system that adheres to the rules that are required of bulk e-mailers. Even with stringent attention to those requirements, you'll still get complaints and, occasionally, be blocked from sending to certain domains. But that's just part of doing business in this new, direct line of communication.

Finally, it goes without saying that every band needs a web site. Make sure that one of the key members of the band registers the domain name, rather than leaving that task to the webmaster. Try and find a hosting service that's located near your residence and within easy access in case of emergency. Get the site set up with a merchant account so that you can sell merchandise, your CD and tickets to your shows. Again, make sure the site is easy to remember, and don't make it a sub-domain of some hosting site. That's lame.

Next to selling out a stadium, the toughest task in music is getting your music played on the radio. And never has it been tougher than it is right now.

Blame the Telecommunications Act of 1996. That Act eased the regulations that limited the number of radio stations any particular company could own in a market, which led to a massive wave of consolidation in the industry, as giants like Clear Channel Communications and Infinity Broadcasting swooped in and bought up the available channels.

What that also did was make it even tougher to get airplay in particular markets, because, all of a sudden, programming decisions were being made on a national basis. Although the decisions on radio airplay haven't been based on individual taste for years—or is it just coincidence that most of the records that get airplay just happened to be backed by multinational corporations?—it exacerbated an existing problem, as formats became ever narrower and playlists tightened.

Yes, there are still some scattered avatars of individualistic programming scattered around the dial. But the operative word is scattered. Unless you're listening late at night or happen to live in a particular listening area, you're cooked.

Fortunately, there is a shining ray of hope amid the gloom. Noncommercial radio, satellite radio and particularly college radio are still largely programmed by individual tastes, so even an act starting out can get some attention for their music.

That's not to say that everything that's sent in gets played. There are still some barriers to overcome on even the freest-form college station. But it's a far cry from the sad state of commercial radio.

Like any other endeavor, it pays to do your homework. Don't send a blues show a tape of your emo band. Find out the shows that a station is broadcasting, find out who makes the decision on what programming goes in, and find out what they like to see from you as an individual. How do you find out? Ask the station. Ask the radio personality. Ask your fellow acts.

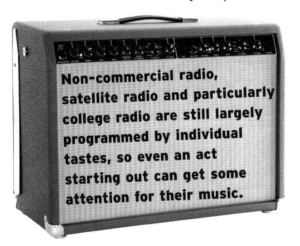

Non-commercial radio, satellite radio and particularly college radio are still largely programmed by individual tastes, so even an act starting out can get some attention for their music.

"Basically, the best way to get music heard at the station is to address a certain programmer," said Debbie Steingesser, the music director of WERS-FM, the Emerson College radio station and one of the most powerful student-run operations in a major market.

"A lot of times I'll get really random packages addressed to me and the record won't even remotely fit into any format of the station. It'll be psychedelic rock or something we just don't play, so it will automatically get thrown out. I really encourage people to check the web site and familiarize themselves with the station and get a feel for what we're doing and then send their record based on the show or the music format they think they fit into."

Once you've determined the right target, you can get your package together. But there are other rules to follow.

Airplay, for instance, works best when it relates to the listener. For instance, if you're playing somewhere in the area where a station's signal reaches, it makes a lot more sense to send in a package mentioning that date than it does if you live 1000 miles away and have no plans to be in the area.

The idea is to build from a slowly expanding circle of airplay that will support your touring and retail sales.

What do you enclose? The elementary rule of the military applies: Keep it simple, Stupid. Two of your press clips, a short bio, and the CD. Do not send a photo unless you want the station staff to write on it and hang it up on the bulletin board. Make sure you note the tour dates in the station's listening area.

It usually helps if you send a jewel box CD as well, because finicky programmers find it too easy to miss the flat envelopes in the stack of things they have on their "to do" list.

Send in your package. Wait a week. Then follow up. If they still haven't gotten to it, wait a week, and then politely follow up. It doesn't hurt to keep badgering as long as you're polite.

Occasionally, you may find it helpful to enlist the services of an independent promotion company. These fine folks have established relationships with the programmers at your target radio stations and spend an inordinate amount of time speaking with them on behalf of their various clients.

While the ability to get airplay varies, the key to these services is they are familiar with whom to contact and how to contact them. The downside is they cost money and there's no guarantee on the results. Some indie promoters are known for specific genres and get great results by tapping into a particularly passionate segment of the market.

Like in publicity, radio promoters are looking for a story. Is the record going to be available? Is the tour active? Is there some type of support going on besides what's on the CD. Even if you don't have a story, the pieces have to be put together in a way that makes sense.

For example, a way to turn off even the hungriest promoter is to say that you're thinking of hiring a publicist, you're looking for distribution, or you're trying to get an in-store date. In other words, have a lot of ifs, buts and maybes in the story.

If you're an established artist and you have a couple records under your belt and you know that you have a record coming up, you should start your game plan for airplay far in advance. It goes without saying that the CD should be finished and not in the demo stage, unless the show targeted specializes in demos. You are making a recording that's intended for airplay; wait until you have the finished product and have laid the groundwork for making sure it's in stores and you have a way to get it out to the masses.

Of course, a local college radio station is going to be much more receptive to a local act than someone from out-of-town. Some of the above rules can slide merely because the programmers know the band and want to help support a local guy.

If you're a national act coming to town, though, it's a good idea to let them know in advance and plan, plan, plan. The biggest hurdle at most radio stations is getting the recording listened to by the staff. After that, if the record is any good, it will likely stand on its own for its shelf life, which is generally a six-week window, unless the band is local and playing frequently in the area.

Satellite radio and certainly Internet radio are also options. The jury is still out on the effectiveness of either one, which are still gaining toeholds with audiences. Still, XM Satellite and Sirius Radio, the two big satellite services, are gaining traction as more and more automobile manufacturers add the service as an option. And with Internet broadcasters taking more time to address specific niche audiences, it's not a bad idea to make friends with a few of the legitimate outlets for music.

Timing is also a big factor in college radio. Semester breaks are sometimes manned by different programmers at some stations. Then there's the inevitable turnover from year to year, as programmers graduate or drop out. By mid-semester, most staffs are dealing with an onslaught of major label records, so attention spans can be limited for unknown acts.

Dropping by the station for a visit can be both a good and bad thing. If you catch someone in the middle of a busy time, you'll get scant attention. If you have a gig in town and set up a station visit in conjunction, it's a good thing.

HOW NOT TO RUIN YOUR MUSIC CAREER

1. Create an affinity group by defining whom you want to reach.
2. Write a marketing plan on obtaining that goal.
3. Set up a place for the community to meet – a web site.

10
THE PITCH

As a participant and observer of the music industry, I've seen the business from both its multinational side and its DIY grassroots. Although far apart in money and scale, the thing they have in common is the "get it" factor.

What's the "get it" factor? In other words, you must "get" that you need to have a short, concise pitch ready at the right moment to approach someone you wish to do business with. And you must recognize when the "right" moment arrives. Not everyone understands or practices that simple tactic, ergo, the ones who do "get it."

Half the battle in determining when that right moment arrives is making the first presentation the correct one.

In most cases, your act will be introduced to others via a recording or live performance, then via a web site, then through references. This applies whether you're going for a gig at a local club, publicity or radio airplay, a performance slot at a festival or for a recording deal or some other means of transmitting your music.

While all are different requests, all require an immediate impact on whomever you refer for more information.

The absolute first thing to understand about your initial point of contact is that whomever you get in touch with is (a) extremely busy;

(b) has more excuses to say no than yes; (c) isn't impressed by rhetoric about how good you think you are; (d) wants to quickly grasp what it is you're all about; and particularly (e) wants to know what's in it for them. And did we mention that they're extremely busy?

Thus, you must pitch them, rather than query them. You must state clearly and succinctly what you are attempting to do and why it's a good thing for them to spend time on.

Think about how things work in sales for the best example of why this approach works. You walk into a car show room and your defenses are up. So what does the good salesman try to do? Not bombard you with high-pressure tactics designed to beat you into submission and achieve *his* objective, i.e., sell you a car.

No, the good salesman works hard to become your friend. He's going to take care of you and make sure you get the best deal possible. You're all brothers-in-arms in this cold, cruel world and he couldn't possibly live with himself if he sold you something that you were not happy about.

The same tactics apply to trying to get your music to the right people. You don't win them over with blather and bull. You present the facts and then leave it to them to decide, maintaining a friendly but persistent and businesslike approach.

The best pitch cuts to the chase: "I have an all-female rock/rap act playing Thursday at 11 p.m. at the Viper Room. They've been getting a lot of press attention in local 'zines. I'd like to invite you to review the show."

No one may be interested in that pitch. But at the least, you've made your case. And even if that particular date or situation is not right for the person, you've planted a seed of recognition, which makes it easier to pitch the next time.

To help you quickly understand what's at stake, the following rules should be applied liberally every two hours until they penetrate the skin:

RULE NUMBER ONE:

The package you put together for anyone should be understood at first glance. At the minimum, whatever you send should have absolutely every bit of contact information contained in a prominent place that won't require a lot of dig-ging. If you're sending a physical object, write it directly on the CD itself and on the outside of the package: Name, phone number, e-mail. Don't make it hard for extremely busy peo-ple to get in touch.

RULE NUMBER TWO:
Understand what they're looking for. It's not too hard to fig-ure out that a nightclub that specializes in bands with names like "Satan's Fury" really won't be interested in a pop singer with two dancers. A bare minimum of homework on this front can save time and money.

RULE NUMBER THREE:
Keep it to the minimum. The contents of your package may vary slightly, depending on whom you're sending the materi-als to and for what purpose. A publicity person would send someone from the media clips from other publications. A radio promoter doesn't need a photo. But the absolute bedrock is the device called, in most cases, a one-sheet. This is a piece of paper that says, clearly and succinctly, who you are, what you do, why you're getting in touch and how to get in touch with you. This piece of paper, along with your music, is all you really need to convey your message. The rest of it speaks for itself.

RULE NUMBER FOUR:
Make your package relatively easy to open without resorting to violence. In most cases, you're sending a CD and a few pieces of paper. There is no need to bind the package in layers of duct tape so that every possible opening is hermetically sealed. Jewel boxes and paper hold up extremely well in most mailing situations within the planetary system and do not need extra binding. More goods have been damaged in opening a stub-born package than have ever been sullied by the postal system.

RULE NUMBER FIVE:

Follow up in a week to ten days. With thousands of packages pouring in over the transom, most decision-makers need a week to sort through it all and make sense. Many need more time. Be polite, be persistent. When is a good time to follow up? That's the most perfect question a supplicant can ask.

RULE NUMBER SIX:

Do not put glitter, streamers or anything else that will instantly fall out of the package and ruin someone's work-space in the package. Rather than enticing them, it will make them mark you for death.

RULE NUMBER SEVEN:

Photos hurt more than help. Radio programmers hate them, as they're concerned with music, not your looks, and most of the people who need to make a decision based on a photo will request them. When you do send a photo, make sure it's clear and in focus. If you submit a blurry, artistic shot, many pub-lications will reject it. Remember that newsprint usually dark-ens a photo. And for God's sake, don't lean against a brick wall, the ultimate artistic outrage.

HOW NOT TO RUIN YOUR MUSIC CAREER

1. Craft a proper approach.
2. Be brief and succinct.
3. Follow up.

11
TOURING

Making a CD is a lot of work; playing live is fun. It's also where the majority of music acts make most of their money, or at least generate the most interest in their work.

The art and science of drawing a crowd has some elements that you can control, others that you cannot. Your time slot will have a lot to do with who comes out to see you. Sunday at midnight is not a great time slot. Friday and Saturday at 10 p.m. is perfect.

The venue you're performing at also has a lot to do with it. Some venues have cache. No matter what, people will go there just because it's...well, it's a place that they like going to. They know that whatever is there, it'll be worth their time and money.

The third item to consider—and perhaps the most important—is the people who run the club. The booker, the sound guy, the bartenders and wait staff, all of them are human beings, subject to the same quirks, foibles, emotions and needs as other human beings. A sure-fire way to destroy your chances of being invited back to a club is to adopt an attitude of disrespect to these folks, drink to excess, and then leave the door open on the way out. Bad news travels fast on the circuit. Even one instance of bad behavior can poison the atmosphere at other local clubs.

There's also the alternative circuit of house concerts, backyards, and rented halls. All of them require a bit more legwork in the setup, and the situation will only be as good as the people running it, but it can be incredibly lucrative and fun if done right.

We'll get back to that in a moment. For starters, let's talk about the traditional touring scene, i.e., playing in a club that offers live music.

Obviously, the more popular the venue, the harder it is to get in the door to schedule a performance. But nothing is impossible if you go about things in a scientific manner.

Your biggest objective in playing out is to draw a crowd. Not just because it's more fun for you to play in front of an audience, although we shouldn't have to tell you that. No, the biggest reason for drawing a crowd is the bar owner is in business to make money. For the night, you're partners with him. Draw well, have a crowd that likes to drink and you'll be invited back. Don't promote your date, draw flies, and it'll be the last night that you play for the bar owner.

It goes without saying that you are a guest in the owner's "home" for that evening. That means treating all the house equipment with respect, not begging for drinks or drink tickets, not making a mess. All of this is duly noted, and it's a small business, with people talking to others in the business frequently to compare notes.

Naturally, anyone starting out in the touring business is going to have to settle for one of the least desirable slots on a multi-band bill and pay their dues. It's just one of those things in life, like death and taxes. But from the very first date, you have a chance to start building something special. It is imperative for anyone involved with your project to get out there and sell, sell, sell. The flier business was built on people like you. Hand 'em out, tack 'em up (but be sure your town won't bust you for putting them up—some places charge $100 a flier) and make sure that everyone knows that if they don't show, they will suffer socially.

The key is not to be in a hurry to play to nobody. If you feel that you can't draw 40-50 people to play a mid-sized room, then you're probably not ready to play a mid-sized room. Most clubs have very little walk-up traffic; your chances of drawing anyone beyond your immediate following are pretty slim for a beginning act.

As such, work out in advance with the club how big a guest list you're going to have. If you're playing for the door, it's hard to turn down the millions of friends who want to get in for free. Many clubs also limit the amount of guests a band can have, even hassling some about the members of the road crew and the girlfriends/boyfriends/assorted hangers-on that travel with your entourage. It's wise to find out in advance all of the details associated with a club's door policy.

Working with other bands is part and parcel of building your following and creating a scene. It's typical that bills are built around bands with a similar draw and following. That creates a party and it typically brings people back. That type of inter-band networking is also a great way to build out from your initial market. Bands from out of town that you're friendly with can recommend you to their local clubs, you can share a bill, and help each other out.

Working with other bands is part and parcel of building your following and creating a scene.

It should be said that the most important element in bringing people out to the shows is your e-mail list. This is your main source of contacting the public in a place where they're likely to see the information. An ad in a local alternative newspaper is nice, but if someone overlooks the ad or quickly turns the page (or worse, never picks up a copy of the news-paper), they're not going to know about the show. An e-mail inbox is something most people check at least once a day. Make sure that you've told them through this process about the show.

Many acts offer discounts on admission with a flier. Since the band is usually playing for whatever they can draw through the door, it takes some bullet biting. But the most beautiful word in the English language is free. The second is discount. You get the picture.

One of the most overlooked aspects of bringing out a crowd to a club is getting your following to come early and stay late. Most clubs that feature independent music typically have three or more bands on a bill. If each band draws 50 people, but the following only shows up and then quickly leaves for each band, the overall impression left by the gathering isn't great.

Once you have established yourselves locally, there will come a time when it's advantageous to stretch out beyond your hometown. The best bands make it into a road-trip for their fans as well as the band. When everyone goes on a grand adventure, it's more fun for everyone. Renting buses and charging all-inclusive tickets is one way to do it. And, where possible, doing your advance work in the town you're traveling to is advisable.

One caveat: realize that you're going to be associated with whomever you play with. If you're on a bill with three bands that are not talented, it's pretty much a certainty that most people will think your band is not talented. If you're a metal band, it doesn't make sense to be on the bill with a tribute to Belle and Sebastian. It's all about building the community of similar birds that want to flock together.

If no one will book you, book yourself. The grand tradition of DIY was born in the backyards of America. A few kegs, a warehouse, some fliers and viola—a night to remember.

The Clarks are a band out of Pittsburgh, PA that built its reputation by constructing a solid regional following for its live shows, then gradually building out its audience.

"For a long time, we focused on our region, almost to the point where we began to be concerned," said Rob James, a guitarist with the band. "We would go to other cities, to Chicago, Cleveland, Washington, D.C., and be playing to nobody. But then over the course of years, what ended up happening was a lot of kids who went to school in Pittsburgh moved away. There are people from Pittsburgh everywhere, or people who have spent time in Pittsburgh that know about the band. So, when we play, it almost becomes a Pittsburgh night. I can't tell you how many times I've gotten people that have come up to me and said, 'Man, I went to Pitt University and I'm originally from here and I've turned all my friends on to your CD and they absolutely love it. I brought all of them out tonight.' Things like that, sort of the classic word-of-mouth, grassroots kind of thing."

As with most bands, the Clarks started out with small goals. "You want to play a certain club on a certain night," said James. "And then you want that night to be successful, so you can get to another night. And from there, those goals kind of escalate to another close metropolis. For us it was always this gradual, slow build, which sometimes became very agonizing. But in retrospect, having those small goals and staying focused on those things that were right in front of us enabled us to do more in the long run."

Jennifer Tefft is a talent booker with Spaceland Productions, which handles a number of prominent nightclubs and concert venues in Los Angeles, including the Henry Fonda Theater.

Tefft is inundated every week with hundreds of packages and e-mails from independent acts looking for a date at one of the Spaceland venues. Choosing which ones will get the nod is part intuition, part packaging, and certainly, having the right credentials on the part of the band.

"If I like them, if they fit musically with a particular night that I'm doing, then it's something I'll consider," said Tefft. "I look for bands making a name for themselves in their town, ones that will grow, that I want to grow with."

To decide which acts to book, Tefft uses a variety of sources, including music-centric magazines and online sites like Pitchfork.

"My favorite way to get material is by e-mail," Tefft said. "I prefer an e-mail press kit with MP3s because I can keep that and re-visit it. If I get a follow-up e-mail or a call or hear about the band from another source, then it's right there in my e-mail and I can find it and access it quickly."

With regular packages, Tefft said, "It might take me weeks or months to get around to listening to it. But with e-mail, I tend to deal with it within 24 hours. Later, you can send a CD with three songs and a bio."

A list of where the band has played before is extremely helpful in making its case. "I look to see which venues they've played in their hometown, because I'm fairly knowledgeable about what the cool venues are in other cities. If they match up with a place similar to ours, it counts a lot."

Of course, drawing well on your initial visit to a venue is important. But the public isn't the only observers that Tefft will listen to.

"I pay attention if the door girl or the bartender says they were really good," Tefft said.

As with other avenues in the music business, doing your homework before approaching a venue is important. Check out its web site, and, if possible, visit the club. Learn what the club or concert hall is about.

"You can answer a lot of questions right away by just looking at the upcoming schedule," said Tefft. "If a touring band is e-mailing about a particular night, they should look it up first to see if it's already booked. And maybe they'll see that the night they were thinking was their target night might not be right, but the night before or after that, they'll see a band that's really appropriate to book them with. Bands that I've never heard of or never seen before are more likely to get shows from me if they e-mail me about specific shows or ideas for whole nights."

Teaming up with a local act is also a great way to make an initial contact, Tefft said.

"Sometimes bands have inspired shows by saying we'd really like to play with Red Krayola. That's what one band did last year, e-mailed about a specific band they wanted to play with. They just liked them, so I made it happen."

O.A.R. (Of A Revolution) is one of the DIY success stories of the last few years.

The band sold over 150,000 copies of its first three albums on its own Everfine Records while allowing fans to freely tape its jam heavy mix of ska, jazz, and rock.

Founding member and drummer Chris Culos said the band stayed involved in all aspects of its business dealings from the very beginning.

"We've developed a pretty strong team," said Culos. "We have a business manager to solve all the financial aspects. And we have David Roberge, our manager, and he's kind of like an A&R guy for us. And then we have our booking agency, CAA, which Dave works very closely with to schedule our tours."

The band's career has evolved, Culos said, "at a comfortable pace. We haven't jumped any steps or anything like that. We started in high school. We recorded a CD for our friends. Then we went off to college and we started spreading the music. Then everyone ended up in college together at Ohio State, and we started playing whenever we could get shows. Anything we could get, fraternity parties, regular parties, bars, anything. And then, once we actually started building a small fan base and wanted to play regularly, that's when Marc's brother, David, stepped in and started organizing the touring a little bit so we could play around our school on the weekends."

"From there," Culos said, "we started playing out a little bit more in the Midwest, but not enough so that it would affect our school work. Marc and I graduated and a couple of the other guys decided to put school on hold so that we could tour full-time. And then we stepped it up a little bit. Our first national tour, we played five nights a week and played in cities we'd never played in before."

Rather than fearing taping, the band encourages it. "It totally helps. It's a way for the audience to take a piece of the night home with them. They come out with some really good equipment. A lot of these kids have formed their own community. We have a message board online and these kids go and find out what shows have been taped and they get in contact with each other. As long as no one's paying for the tapes, they'll trade for other bands or shows. So people who never even knew each other will make friends and meet up at the show, get each other rides. It's really incredible to see this community that's formed between the kids on the message boards who come out and tape shows. We're now close friends with a lot of them."

Once your act establishes a bit of a name in your region or city, you can begin to define your audience in ways that may attract sponsors who seek to reach a similar demographic.

The Clarks built upon their strong identification with the Pittsburgh area. Your act may rely on other traits. Is your audience made up of college graduates in their mid to late '20s who enjoy a particular regional type of beer and have disposable income? Are they lesbian feminists who strongly identify with the empowering lyrics of your music? Do you have a strong following of super models who are highly fashion-conscious?

If you bring them together on a regular basis, you might be able to draw a local sponsor who's interested in reaching such an audience and bringing them over to their restaurant. Or a liquor sponsor who wants to cultivate that audience and get them to try a new product. Today, advertisers are particularly interested in reaching out in a peer-to-peer fashion to they type of audiences that go out to hear live music. You can build a compelling case that your audience is one that they should be interested in.

A word of caution: even if you have a strong following in your particular city, it's highly unlikely that you will immediately attract the attention of a national advertiser—unlikely, but not impossible. It's best to concentrate on the sort of local business that can benefit and be patronized in measurable ways by your audience.

Once you've established that particular city, you can move on to larger audiences.

Sponsorship is no longer such an odious thing to musicians, but there is still a stigma attached to outright shilling in some quarters. Fear not that there's too much compromisin' on the road to your horizon. Some corporations actually don't want to sell too hard.

"I think from both sides there's been a tremendous stand-down from what used to be required," said John Pantle, an agent with The Agency Group in Los Angeles. "Advertising and sponsorship used to be, 'Hey, I'm so and so,' and then a picture of you holding up a bottle of whatever. Nowadays, it's very different."

Pantle recalled telling one major sponsor that a band he repre-sented wanted nothing to do with sponsorships. They would not allow banners on stage. They would not be photographed using the prod-uct. They didn't want to be associated with the product. The band still got the sponsorship. Why? Because the audience that came out to hear them was defined and desirable to the company.

HOW NOT TO RUIN YOUR MUSIC CAREER

1. Develop your e-mail list.
2. Do your homework before approaching a venue.
3. Encourage your following to come early and stay late.

12
THE ONLINE WARS

It was near the end of an hour of talk radio when Miles Copeland was asked by NPR host Warren Olney for his final thoughts on the traditional record industry's reaction to digital music technology.

Copeland, the owner of Ark21 Records, the founder of the legendary IRS Records, and the former manager of Sting, didn't hesitate. The record industry, Copeland said, took the same approach to digital music as British Prime Minister Neville Chamberlain did with his infamous appeasement of Adolph Hitler just before World War II.

"We all buried our heads in the sand and said it would all be okay," said Copeland. "And it was not okay. I don't see how we can fight technology. I, as a company, cannot fight free. You have to face the fact at some point that it's going to be a losing battle. The average person will get (music) for free, whether we like it or not."

That, in a nutshell, is what's facing the recorded music industry as it enters the online sales era. You can't fight free. An entire generation of teenagers has grown up knowing that virtually any track from any album is available online at no cost.

A prominent executive from one of the nation's largest retailers puts it this way: "We've lost an entire generation. I just tell people to skip them, forget about them, because we're never going to get them back. Let's work on the next generation. There's some hope that we can train them."

Toward that end, and in a manner not unlike another famous British prime minister, Winston Churchill, the major recording industry has decided to take on the world with a stiff upper lip and an alternative to free: paid subscription services.

You can't fight free. An entire generation of teenagers has grown up knowing that virtually any track from any album is available online at no cost.

Ah, but here's the rub: just as the industry finally prepares to offer a digital music jukebox that will mimic the best features of Napster, the most wildly popular file-swapping software ever created, while eliminating its worst feature—that it gives music away for free—the government has taken an interest.

While all of the investigations are likely to have been placed on the back-burner because of the traumatic events of Sept. 11, their instigation might remind historians of another wartime analogy, this time to Vietnam. For while the major recording labels keep hoping they can declare victory and get out of the battles of the digital music revolution, they instead find themselves increasingly bogged down in a war they cannot win.

It was five years ago, on a steamy New York summer day, that Hilary Rosen, then head of the Recording Industry Association of America, the U.S. record industry's largest trade group, sat before an audience composed largely of peers and remarked that "piracy is no longer an issue."

"I can't seem to find anybody to stop talking about piracy," said Rosen, speaking at the Plug-In '99 convention sponsored by Jupiter

Communications, a New York research firm. "I don't know if anybody has noticed, but I don't talk about it any more. As a practical matter I don't think we are in a pirate marketplace. I think we are in a place where there are a lot of other things to do and talk about, and piracy, as it were, is really not a significant concern."

But as Rosen soon learned, technology can never be conquered; it always moves forward.

To be fair, Rosen had every reason to believe at that moment that her organization had a handle on the piracy problem. Its learning curve appeared to be gathering momentum after a rocky start.

The RIAA had been late to discover the file-swapping activities going on in the computer world. Relying on a network of retired detectives, it had concentrated its efforts on illegal bootlegging operations that were selling physical goods at flea markets, car washes, and other out-of-the-way corners of the counterfeit retailing world.

But after younger RIAA staffers began telling their superiors that you could obtain just about any song you wanted online, the organization woke up and began to pay attention to the Internet. What they found appalled them: a parallel universe where entire albums could be duplicated and sent to an international audience at the click of a mouse. And it was already spinning out of control.

Marshalling its resources, the RIAA quickly began to plot a strategy that was one part saber-rattle, one part education, and one part litigation.

By July, 1999, the RIAA had ramped up its monitoring of the online marketplace, notifying Internet service providers of pirated recordings on their systems and helping to devise and launch what they believed were two powerful weapons against online aggressors: the Secure Digital Music Initiative and the Digital Millennium Copyright Act.

While the activities were not seen as a perfect solution to copyright problems, they were steps that would conceivably drive file swapping back into the underground and perhaps make those who attempted to do it wary of the consequences of their actions.

Then, Napster arrived, followed shortly thereafter by the MP3.com Beam-it service. Suddenly, technology had thwarted the Maginot Line erected by the record industry.

Both Napster and MP3.com argued that they were not copyright infringers, but merely provided a forum where people could exchange information and tools to showcase products that they already owned, both perfectly permissible under existing laws.

As history has shown, the court system did not buy those arguments. But while the cases were being played out in the courts, technology advanced again, birthing Gnutella, Freenet and other file-swapping services. These services were harder, if not nearly impossible to trade, and thus were more immune to litigation than Napster and MP3.com.

At that point, digital music became the equivalent of a dike with a thousand leaks, leaving the RIAA resembling a Dutch boy sticking his finger in the dike and hoping to grow more digits. And it was then that another solution arose: establish a legitimate online music marketplace.

The major recording labels have been discussing the dream of digital music for some time, although it was only recently that efforts went beyond mere lip service.

Many executives quietly hoped that they would be retired when the issues of delivering music directly to consumers surfaced, thus missing the thorny dilemmas posed by a new system that has the potential to totally restructure the business practices of the modern recording corporation.

What could veteran executives say to their long-time customers, the retailers, when the time came for digital music? How would it affect manufacturing and distribution, areas that have long provided a source of profits both on and off the books?

Yet when the time came for action, the record industry moved decisively.

Beleaguered Napster received a cash infusion and alliance with Bertelsmann; MP3.com was purchased by Vivendi; Real Networks and Microsoft, the dominant media players in the marketplace, began designing their own subscription plans in conjunction with major record labels; and AOL and Yahoo! began plans for their own digital subscription services.

Despite early promises that the Web would level the playing field by creating an equal-access pipeline, each of the major record distributors that controlled retail and radio channels over the last 10 years quickly began taking substantial stakes or signed complicated licensing arrangements with the key revenue-generating outlets reaching the vast majority of the music audience on the Net. Thus, the digital music revolution shifted once again.

Instead of competing for shelf space and airtime, the battle that is now going on is one for the hearts and minds of the online population, a group that has grown used to getting music for free.

Slowly, the sites that the online community visits for news, videos, and promotional items will gradually tie in the digital subscription services, stealthily penetrating the active audience already captured by such sites. The hope is that they can convert customers used to getting music for free into paying customers.

Your decision on whether to permit others to possess your music for free or purchase it online is strictly a business call.

Both models have successful revenue streams attached to them. You can give away your music and make money from the expanded opportunities to sell that crowd merchandise, subscriptions, tickets and, yes, CDs. Or you can rely on selling the protected digital files and try to grow that into a lucrative revenue stream.

As we'll see in the next chapter, the biggest enemy of unknown bands is that they are, in fact, unknown. If you develop a large fan base, there are any number of ways to capitalize and create revenue from that base.

If no one knows who you are, then you will have to be content with selling two or three digital files online.

HOW NOT TO RUIN YOUR MUSIC CAREER

1. Don't fear the online world – embrace it.

13
RETAIL AND DIRECT SALES

Although the record retailing side of the business has taken some hits over the last few years, it still figures to be part of the entertainment scene for the next decade in some form or another.

Whether or not there are discs being sold in the various racks in the store really doesn't matter much to the retailer. They make a great deal of their money from what's called price and positioning. In other words, they get CDs and DVDs at special deals and mark them up, and sell the space on the walls and at the ends of the aisles. If the business becomes all digital and CDs vanish, savvy retailers will still exist by creating an environment conducive to hanging out and loading your digital playback device.

If you've been paying attention, you've also noticed a good number of retailers selling cappuccino, merchandise, magazines, newspapers, funny toys, greeting cards and any other number of non-musical items. Clearly, those stores are selling ambience, not discs.

As the popularity of the iPod and other listening devices increases, the major retailing giants of the last four decades will likely rely more and more on the other items, squeezing what they carry in their stores even more.

But there still are a number of thriving independent record stores that cater to a discriminating audience that wants to come in, hang out, and check out what's new. As the enduring popularity of vinyl will tell you, the medium may change, but the need to gather and discuss music in an atmosphere that serves to honor it will remain the same. You may be filling up your iPod at a listening station, but fill it up you will.

For now, let's concentrate on the CD, still the dominant way to deliver music.

Most indie stores will work with you on a consignment basis for your CD. It's not a magic trick to get in there. Just walk in the store, find the right person to speak to, and then ask. It'll likely be no more than one or more CDs, but you will be on sale and have a presence in the market.

Most of the smaller independent and self-published artists sell directly to fans, either through an online retailer or directly at gigs and their own web sites. The process for signing up for an outside vendor's online site is fairly simple, but beware of whom you're dealing with. Some online stores and distributors have gone out of business owing their labels and self-published musicians money and many hundreds of units of CDs. Good luck getting them back.

One of the major success stories of the DIY revolution online has been CDBaby, a Portland-based online retailer that has specialized in independent and self-published musicians.

The site quickly took on a life of its own, becoming a major hub for online sales and a destination where fans of new music can turn to find interesting projects.

CDBaby developed its reputation by being fair and upfront with its customers (imagine that in the entertainment biz!). It delivers on its promises and has sold over $10 million in independent music CDs in a faltering marketplace, no easy task.

In the process of building his business, Derek Sivers became something of a white knight to the beleaguered independent music community and a fixture at many music industry conventions (including the DIY Convention, where he has delivered a benediction on being a musician for several years).

His philosophy of success stems from a chance encounter with a well-known producer, whom he declines to identify.

"Back when I was promoting my record in 1996 or so, I was just kind of sending my package out everywhere," said Sivers. "And one day this really successful, well-known producer called up. He happened to be in somebody's office, saw the package there on the desk, picked it up, looked through it, and said, "Hmmm. The guy's got his shit together." And I guess he just had some time on his hands and picked up the phone and called me."

The producer quickly adopted Sivers, imparting his hard-won wisdom from 30 years in the record business.

From those conversations, Sivers distilled his own philosophy of success.

"I find that a lot of musicians are kind of like college students who are going out into the world for the first time, where you think that the way things were in college, where if you just study hard and do well on your tests, that you'll excel. They get out of college thinking that the world will be like that, and they're kind of shocked to find out that it's not. I think a lot of musicians are in that same boat, kind of thinking that if they just write the best songs and play the best guitar and have the tightest arrangements, that it will all just fall into place with them and make it out into the world and find out—to continue the metaphor—it's much more like high school, where it's all about who you know and being cool and being in certain cliques."

The unfairness of the world crushes many musicians, Sivers noted.

"That's why every musician throughout history has always made fun of whatever the teen pop star is at the time because 'They suck. We rule.' And 'why are they millionaires and we're not?' I think the reason that there have been more pop stars on the charts that came from art school than came from music school is that sometimes if you're too focused on the music itself, you forget that the pop world has always surrounded the image, identifying with a role model up there on stage who happens to be singing."

Sivers has the same problem himself when trying to define CDBaby's success.

"I've never really understood why CDBaby seemed to be more popular than other sites. At first, we were the only ones doing it, but as time went on, there were other options that people had, but people seem to like CDBaby the best, and I'm never sure why. Here's one idea: I think people can read between the lines when they see a business doing something only for the profit, or only as a business with a capital B. When somebody's doing something—and I really mean like the kind of operation if I was going to find somebody to do a FilmBaby type thing—that it would have to come out of wanting to do this whether it made any money or not, and then letting the money happen if it does, kind of like the book titled *Do What You Love, The Money Will Follow.* You would have to come from that point of view to be successful. You can tell when somebody's doing something only as, 'hey, let's make some money off these musicians.' That philosophy, I mean, it's a little strange. Even if it's other businesses that are trying to hook up with CDBaby, you hear that unspoken philosophy behind what they're doing. 'Yeah, we'll make some money off these people trying to become successful.' And even if they hide it well, I think you can smell it."

One of the major points addressed by Sivers is worthy of consideration when pondering whether to put your music online.

Sivers noted that the biggest enemy of musicians is not piracy, the red flag waved by the bigger companies in the music industry as a threat to the survival of life on this planet.

The biggest enemy of musicians is obscurity.

Don't listen to the wailing and gnashing of teeth by the big record labels over file-sharing and peer-to-peer systems and the like. Did you know that such complaints about technology have been going on since the days of piano rolls? It's true. The big music publishing companies of yore were worried that the piano rolls would cut into sales of sheet music. They lobbied for a tax on these mechanical marvels. Hence, the name "mechanicals" has been attached to such reproduction royalties.

The same arguments about the end of life as we know it on the planet were raised when FM radio arrived; and when the digital audio tape and the compact disc were born; and, as anyone who has been following the Napster saga and the other online tales knows, the same crisis mode has again gripped the recorded music industry, causing it to worry that its expense account lunches will have to be taken at chain restaurants. The horror, the horror.

As in the past, most observers of technological change expect the music industry to adapt to changing times and eventually embrace online services. Some argue that compulsory licensing to various services will become the standard, wherein an online service pays a fee for the use of all music and apportions it to the various master rights holders.

Complaints about technology have been going on since the days of piano rolls.

Whatever and whenever something happens, it won't change the basic argument for the musician who is largely trying to concentrate on building his or her own business.

Now that distribution has been largely solved by the advent of the World Wide Web and its ability to transmit MP3 files to anywhere in the world, the biggest previous advantage of major companies over individuals has been overcome.

But the next biggest barrier to actually distributing your music has traditionally been its marketing. Let's do the math and we'll see how daunting a task it is to rise above the clutter of that many releases.

There are roughly 30,000-60,000 albums released in any given year by the majors, independents and DIY artists around the world. Those are generally accepted numbers, since no one keeps track of every single bit of music that's released. That figure doesn't count remixes or the constantly circulating tapes from live shows, rehearsals, and jam sessions that ardent music fans seek out.

There are 365 days a year. That means there are 8760 hours per year. Let's say the average CD on those releases holds 60 minutes of music. That means, even at the low end of 30,000 albums per year, someone who wanted to listen to all of the albums would need 180,000 hours.

Clearly, it's an uphill battle for the brief attention span that will be allotted to listening to music. Therefore, there has to be a compelling reason for someone to take the time to listen to your album. It may be a friend's recommendation; it may be something they heard at a show; it may be based on a review.

Or...it may be that someone on one of the online music sites is a fan and is trying to turn others on to your music. So why wouldn't you want to take advantage of that opportunity, particularly since your competition includes many albums whose multinational corporate backers are spending upwards of a million dollars on promoting and marketing and publicizing those albums in an attempt to steer listener attention?

The arguments put up by the major labels regarding copyright issues and their artists sound compelling. But understand one thing: they are protecting their own interests, not necessarily yours. And their interest is maintaining absolute control over the copyrights that they have under their control.

Michael Weiss, the CEO of Morpheus, an online music P2P service, told of the attitude concerning attempts to get music online at a DIY Convention in New York.

"I went to the record labels five years ago and said, 'Look, we need to license your music to put it out on a subscription service online.' And all five of them said, 'Mike, it's going to be a cold day in hell before we ever let our music go out online on a subscription service.'"

While that cold day in hell has inevitably arrived in the form of iTunes and other services, no service yet has every available piece of music in existence. And none of the services has yet proved that consumer loyalty will be retained over the long haul.

Because you have to grab every opportunity that's available to you at the beginning of your career, you must consider P2P as another outlet for your music. You have time after that to sit down and debate the merits of digital rights management and the justice of allowing your music to be listened to without direct compensation to you. Today, your biggest enemy is that no one will hear your music.

There are many online services to consider in your quest to capture the ears of the world. It's wise to look at them as you would any store. If a customer enters that store, you want to have your music available in as many of them as you can afford to be in, just on the off-chance that someone will be turned on to your music and wish to purchase it.

But it's also wise to consider releasing your MP3 files to several of the online services that allow widespread music swapping without any compensation. The ability to get feedback on your music and start to build a buzz is what such tactics are all about. Many peer to peer systems are monitored by services that are seeking to track illegal activity and to measure what's popular.

It's not unheard of for an artist to attract attention by popping up on the radar screen as a frequently traded file. Such acts as O.A.R. and any number of jam bands that allowed their music to freely circulate built up enormous regional and then national followings by allowing their music to be freely traded. And while the improvisational nature of jam band music made capturing specific performances an obsession with their fan base, it's arguable that any music that an artist is trying to gain attention for can be leveraged in similar fashion. After all, there are official CDs to be sold, complete with album artwork and packaging; merchandise; live gigs; other art (videos, films, books) to be up-sold. It's all up to you.

But first, you have to intrigue the customer. And that's where your music comes in.

Rory Felton is a co-founder of the Militia Group, a successful punk label in Southern California. They had great success with their first record, selling 55,000 copies.

"I think one real key was the band has a huge Internet fan base," says Felton. "They were really on top of e-mailing, really on top of just talking to their fans, whether it was over IM or at shows or whatever. And it was just a really big spreading of the word."

What separates those who are successful in online sales from those who are not?

"It's definitely not the quality of the music," says Sivers. "Some of my favorite records on CDBaby, I just can't get anybody to buy a copy. Often, whenever somebody's a top-seller on CDBaby, I go visit their web site or I call them up and ask what they're doing. And usually, it just comes down to a matter of effort. They're out there being very persistent and constantly going for the sale, doing things that are directly focused on CD sales instead of just beating around the bush or hoping people come up to them on stage and ask, 'Hey, where can I get your CD?' These are the ones that are out in the audience saying, 'Here it is. Buy it. You don't have cash? We have a credit card machine.' Or they have a friend work the audience while they're on stage."

Working the crowd is also an art. Clearly, having your cousin Otis bring the CD around is a bad choice. Consider hiring someone attractive and personable if no one in your inner circle fits that description.

Sivers concurs. "I've heard from two people now that they actually hired a model to work the crowd at the gig and they said they did amazingly well. You can hire a model and she'll work for $150, and it's worth it. They sold $500 in CDs because they hired a model to work the crowd."

The reason such tactics work? Draw on your own experiences. Are you more likely to buy something when approached in a friendly manner by an attractive person? Or will you wander by the merchandise table, abandoning your chair or key position, in order to spend money? It's an impulse buy.

Another effective tactic is to hand out a flier at the show to every member of the audience. The flier would read: "If you didn't bring any cash to the gig, go to (your online site) tonight and pick up the CD online." People who didn't have money on the night of the show will then be able to pick it up afterwards.

CDBaby actually asks its customers where they heard of the artist. "And so many times on Sunday and Monday we'd get: 'Went to the show;' 'didn't have any cash;' 'got a flier;' 'Came here to buy it,' said Sivers.

The direct approach also works well with independent retailers. These are the mom-and-pop stores that are the lifeblood of the indie musician. They are dedicated to promoting and exploring all forms of new music and are typically run by people who are immersed in their local scenes.

Todd Clifford is a local retailer in Los Angeles who runs Sea Level Records. He advises that someone walk into the store and ask to sell it there.

"That is actually the best way to get my attention," Clifford said. "I get a lot of things in the mail. A lot of the problems we have with bands are when they're not from Los Angeles, they have no choice but to send it to me. But the best thing for me is to have you come in and see what our store is about and know if it would fit with what you're trying to do. Otherwise, if you send it to us just because we're an option, we might not be doing what you're trying to do. And someone else might be better for it. It's kind of wasting efforts on all parts."

Your biggest enemy isn't piracy – it's obscurity.

Once again, kindness and courtesy goes a long way toward making things happen. Remember the store clerk above all.

"When somebody brings in a consignment CD, they sometimes don't remember to give me one," said Clifford. "And when someone asks me what it sounds like, I have to say, 'I have no idea.' And chances are, they don't purchase that one."

Price is an important consideration as well. If you are a local artist competing with a $19.98 list price CD, you may win the battle for the sale if yours is priced at $10.

The best way to research what works and what doesn't in a retail environment is simple: visit a few stores in your area. If the clerks aren't incredibly busy, ask a few questions about what's selling in the store, and then decide if going to the time and trouble of having your recording in that store is worth it. You may very well decide to stick with direct sales. But you will have made an informed decision about the possibilities of doing it.

HOW NOT TO RUIN YOUR MUSIC CAREER

1. Your biggest enemy isn't piracy – it's obscurity.
2. Visit your local retailer and get to know them personally.

14
HOUSE CONCERTS

Besides the usual nightclubs, concert halls, bars and gazebos, there is a growing movement toward house concerts.

The beauty of the house concert is it's entertainment in its purest form. Unlike a nightclub, the rules are pretty much whatever you wish them to be. You can request no smoking, no drinking, you don't need a lot of equipment or a huge sound system, you can start at whatever time you wish and end whenever.

But the biggest reason for doing them is that the audience is there for you, not to chat up members of the opposite sex, drink or do the many hundreds of annoying things people do in bars when you're performing.

A house concert does not necessarily take place in a living room, although that's usually the first choice. Barns, basements, pastures, and backyards are popular forums for the event. Suitability is the key consideration—a four-piece rock band works a lot better in a barn than in a living room. Similarly, a wispy acoustic performer is better off in front of a living room audience than a pasture.

But in urban environments, the apartment center or hall have become the performing venue of choice.

The process for house concerts is pretty well understood by the participants. Typically, a fan of the music decides that they want to turn other people they know on to the artist. They decide to contact the artist and set up a house concert. The deal works like this: the artist is typically guaranteed a certain amount of money. A door charge is instituted. Food or drink may or may not be a part of the deal.

The artist comes, performs, gets a chance to sell the new CD and merchandise, mingles with new-won fans, and gets a cut of the door (typically more than half, although generous patrons, particularly those who have been hitting the wine during the show, have been known to fork over the entire bankroll).

Always ask for an intermission at your house concert. Not only is it tough to sustain attention for long periods in such an intimate venue, but it also provides the opportunity to up-sell the audience on your new CD and merchandise. Most house concert patrons will be only too glad to take advantage of the opportunity to support an artist that they've built a strong connection with over the last 45 minutes. In the chaos of a gig ending, many of them may slip out the door before buying. At half time, they're focused and motivated.

Naturally, performing in a non-traditional venue has its drawbacks. You may have to lug your equipment up several flights of stairs. In an apartment building, you can't crank up the volume to coliseum levels. The room you perform in may not be acoustically perfect, and you may find yourself seated on a stool that's great for holding a plant, but certainly uncomfortable for a performer.

You may also, given that most houses do not come equipped with a stage, find yourself in uncomfortably close proximity to the guests. While this creates a certain sense of intimacy, it also breaks down some barriers that you may or may not be willing to see fall. This is particularly true of those who have been hitting the wine during the show. Remember, they won't be carrying on in the way that people do in a public venue. You'll have to entertain them for two hours in close proximity. You'll get to know them in ways other venues simply can't provide.

Despite those caveats, the shows can be a great way to spend an evening entertaining anywhere from 25-50 or more people in a setting where the artist is usually treated with reverence. Unlike a birthday party or other gig, they're there to hear you, not to tune you out as background noise.

There are any number of organizations across the country that cater to house concerts. Usually, putting the word out to your fan base can generate some attention. Most house concerts are generated by word of mouth connections and attract an audience of friends and family.

The house concert is usually performed away from your usual performance areas. Thus, seeing the "venue" may occur for the first time when you walk in the door. Like any performing situation, it's wise to set up the ground rules up front. Plan out who will introduce you, the break, what is available in the facility and what is expected. Get it in writing.

Like any club date, the settlement can go smoothly or can be a time for finger pointing and debate. Door takes should be managed by someone in your entourage if at all possible.

HOW NOT TO RUIN YOUR MUSIC CAREER

1. House concerts are more intimate than arenas. Develop your ability to talk to your audience.

2. You are a guest in someone's home. Nothing will make them happier than doing a little homework and throwing in some references to the house and the people in the audience.

15
THE AGE BARRIER

In certain cultures, age means experience, wisdom, veneration, a golden period of shared knowledge; in show business, age is the creeping death that knocks on the door of hope.

Like athletes and actors, musicians are perceived to have a set shelf life. There is a general perception that a major label artist needs to be no older than age 26 in order to launch a career.

Why? Because the time and investment cycle on a major label release is three years, majors generally try to estimate how many records they will gain from an artist down the road that will still be fruitful. The thinking is that an artist that is in their mid-30s begins to lose appeal to the prime 16-26 year old marketplace, the trend-setting group that largely determines the sway of popular music.

The age 26 barrier is, of course, arbitrary; all the more surprising because few, if any, major label acts survive beyond the initial album release. Without significant success it's one and done, making an age restriction even more ludicrous.

While it is true that certain physical skills diminish with age—your ability to sing on key can warble after age 46 and dexterity diminishes—much can be overcome with repetition and constant work on your skills. Cunning and knowing your own body makes up for any minor slippage.

But the one barrier that is hardest to overcome is perception. And that barrier does exist at the upper levels of the music business, one of the innumerable risk versus reward measurements calculated by multinational recording companies that plan to invest significant time and corporate resources on a career.

While such prejudice can be overcome by the usual methods—looking younger than your age, airbrushing and outright lying—age can be a significant barrier to any investment by an outside source.

Now, this is not to say that exceptions to the rule don't exist. Artists are found on many independent labels whose birthday falls before the early 1980s, and certain genres of music (blues, folk and world music spring immediately to mind) are less susceptible to the prejudice. A 40-year-old bluesman or woman is practically a teenager!

Fortunately, the DIY approach to music making is age agnostic. As long as you can muster a crowd and have the energy to fulfill the multitudinous tasks that go into being a performer, you can build a career. Your act is less sensitive to age-related demographics because you're aiming at a smaller core audience, one that supports your art because they like it and they like you.

That affinity doesn't come with an expiration date.

Dick Dale is the acknowledged inventor of surf rock, which he continues to practice well into his 60s.

He remains a staunch DIY'er.

"The reason I'm considered the bad guy, the maniac, the guy who's difficult to work with, is because I know how they steal. I know what they do. And so I'd rather be a big fish in a little pond than play the big fucking game. I won't go for it. I won't stand for it. And they all know it."

In the beginning of his career, Dale didn't understand how the game was played.

"I would see the payola. Same thing today. You want to be a rock 'n roll star? Spend a million dollars and anybody can be a rock 'n roll star. Just buy your way onto the cover of *Rolling Stone* or any major magazine. And that's how it's done. Your product is only as good as your marketing ability. Look at the pet rock, for Christ's sake! I even bought one. That's the way it's done. Today, kids sign up with a major label and the rights to their music are gone forever; owned by the company. Now, if you haven't paid off what they call tour support, the money put into promoting your record in the first four months, you don't ever see a dime. So, it's bullshit. I've seen it happen over and over. Courtney Love said it as beautiful as could be done in an e-mail across the nation. She said the same thing I've been saying for the last 25 years. So I said fuck that stuff. And the major promoters won't work with Dick Dale because they say he's too difficult to work with. Oh, really? Why don't you try telling the truth one time!

"So if Dick Dale says he's going to be someplace, I'm going to be someplace. And there's no lying, no bullshit. And if I fail, it's only because of the mistakes that I made, not anybody else. And no one else is going to blame anybody else. So that's what I do. I do it all myself. I just say hey, they know how to find me."

HOW NOT TO RUIN YOUR MUSIC CAREER

1. Don't buy into other people's notions of who you are.

16
CROSSING OVER TO FILM, BOOKS AND BEYOND

While a musician's primary goal is to make music, it must be said that creative people usually aren't limited in the areas of their creativity to one niche. Now, more than ever, the ease of production in film, books, and other art forms has led musicians to explore different areas of their creative side.

The most obvious area of crossing over is on the video side. Many bands begin chronicling their careers via video at the very early stages. Not only is it a great idea to do so if the band is successful, but such footage can also be useful if a band member becomes a star in another incarnation, or for future documentarians who want footage from a particular scene or time that captures the flavor of the moment.

Video is particularly appealing to the growing audience with a broadband connection to the Internet. Music videos are among the most popular streaming media on the net. They're quick entertainment to an attention-deficient audience at home and work.

Any small, hand-held video camera with a decent picture can be used for the operation. It's a good idea to invest in a tri-pod at some point, if only to vary the trembling hand-held look that even the steadiest hand produces.

The footage can be incorporated into a separate release by the band via DVD for not much more money than a regular CD costs. And the footage can also be used for backstage glimpses on your web site.

Crossing over in the literary world is also a possibility. A compilation combining the band's lyrics and artwork makes a nice addition to any merchandising package that you can sell at the gigs or on the web site. Many print-on-demand packages for books are around $500, giving you a solid presentation and yet another revenue stream.

Traditional merchandise—t-shirts and other wearables— have also come down in price over the years, although still cost anywhere from $1 a shirt on up, depending on make, style, and art work. You should always keep your merchandise in mind when designing a logo. Great artwork on a wearable can lead to, at the least, a lot of free promotion of your act.

17
THE LONG RIDE DOWN

There comes a time in every act's career where the hits stop coming, the panties no longer hit the stage, and the booking agents have you sharing a dressing room next to the mule pen at the county fair.

Yes, popularity is a fickle thing. The ride down is often a cruel time, as any number of stories on VH1 will tell you. It often arrives without warning, as the momentum train slows into the station without a conductor's voice telling you to get off.

"As far back as I could remember, I always wanted to be a rock star," said Pat DiNizio of the Smithereens. "Everybody tried to talk me out of it. I wouldn't listen to anybody. But basically, where I'm coming from, just being a working-class kid from New Jersey who was a garbage man until he was 30 years old, the first thing I would advise you is don't listen to what anyone has to tell you, because there are people who are out there who would conspire just to dash your dream."

DiNizio was talking about perseverance on the way up. But it also requires a good deal of energy and attention to detail to help yourself on the way down.

The biggest lesson is to focus not on what you lost, but what you gain.

Aimee Mann is one artist who has triumphed in the face of adversity.

"You know, somebody who sells 200,000 records is beneath the notice of most of the people in the business because the business is so oriented to multi-platinum records now," she said. "That leaves a lot of really talented people who sell significant amounts of records kind of out in the cold, and the only place they can go is the indie route."

If you've followed the advice in this book, you've made a ton of connections, have established a good reputation, and still control the music that you've created. You can still work the licensing angles with your catalog, can still play a certain number of times a year without burning out your aging or increasingly distracted audience, and may decide to move into any of a number of ancillary careers that have more to do with the behind-the-scenes aspects of the music business than the upfront glamour.

There's also the possibility that your career could morph in a direction that you didn't plan.

Delbert McClinton is a veteran blues rocker of major and independent labels. He now makes a highly lucrative living sponsoring blues cruises.

"Before I started my cruise, I played two years in a row for another," he recalled. "And I love blues music, but to be trapped on a boat for a week with a lot of mediocre blues is a hard gig. So I talked with this friend of mine and told him I thought I could do a better job of this and have more of an eclectic lineup. So we started doing it, and the first two years we had to eat it. Then it started to pay back a little bit of what we had put into it. And it's just about paid everything back and doing really well. I've had so many people say, 'I don't care where we go. We can go out six miles into the ocean and drop anchor, and that's fine.' The reason I started doing this was the opportunity to get a vacation with a lot of my friends that I don't get to see and get us all together for a week once a year, and what's a better place than in the Caribbean on a ship?"

But what happens if you get sent to that music industry desert island, that place of exile that no one returns from? One DIYer was sent there early in his career. He has survived and lived to tell the tale.

Imagine, if you will, that you have achieved everything in your career that you desired: worldwide fame, a Grammy, a multi-platinum record.

Then imagine that it's all taken away by one of the biggest scandals in music industry history.

That's what faced Fabrice Morvan of Milli Vanilli. And what did he do? He picked up a guitar and reinvented his career.

"The minute everything went down with Milli Vanilli, in my mind, I said to myself, 'Look. I don't know what's going to happen, but I have a dream. And my dream is to become a singer-songwriter. I don't know how I'm going to get there, but I'm going to work really hard. I don't know how hard it's going to be, but I'm going to do it, because this is what I want to do. I strayed away, but I'm going to get there. And I don't know what to expect.' With that same idea, that's how I started the process."

Do you have a philosophy of life?

"My philosophy of life is whatever happens as a human being, try to stay as positive as possible, even if it's a very difficult thing to do in hard times, because being negative just will pull you down all the time. So staying positive as much as you can is one thing. Another thing, as an artist, don't listen to whatever people are saying to you. 'Oh, man, you're crazy! You're going to do that? No, I don't think that's possible!' No, just believe in yourself. Keep nurturing whatever talent you have, try to get there and try to progress and try to evolve. It's a very important thing as an artist. And you'll see that the more you work on yourself, the stronger and more confidence you'll gain. That's what happened to me. By getting better all the time and progressing with the music, with the idea, with the concept, with the songwriting, trying to get to it right away and capture their attention, that's very important.

"I've done a lot of things and a lot of people are aware that I am here, that I'm doing music, so it never stops. It never stops. I keep going and then when the time comes, when I finally have product in the stores, more people will remember. It's about touching. There's no paid advertising here; it's a grassroots campaign and it's very personal. I want people to get a sense of me. I don't block anybody.

People want to talk to me about the past, I'll talk about the past; on the plane, in the street, whatever."

Fabrice vowed to live his life differently in this incarnation of his career.

"Oh, hell, man," he said, laughing. "You know, the first time, they call it first fame. When you get exposed to your first thing, you're buck wild, man! I was a young kid, out of control, marinating in testosterone, no parental supervision or anything. So you go nuts, you go crazy. It was fun! But I'm glad it's behind me now, you know? For me, it's about getting better, it's about the music, really. Developing, getting better, and then coming out with something special and do the best you can."

Perhaps one of the greatest stories about DIYing was told by Wayne Kramer at the 2003 DIY Convention.

Kramer actually had to overcome prison to achieve his career.

"There was a moment of doubt at the end of the MC5. 'Well, now what? What do I do?' I was 24 years old, and what happened is, I didn't handle it well and I turned to a life of crime, and I paid a great price for that. But what came out of it was that I had to redefine success.

"Success is being able to continue to do this thing that I love to do and that's really at the core of what DIY is all about. You find something that you're passionate about and then do what you've got to do to make that happen.

"Take the position of leadership to make something happen, to lift the people's spirits around you up out of the complacency of complaining, and do something about it. Make something happen, take that responsibility.

"DIY means being a collaborator. It doesn't mean I'm in it all by myself in the world and I've got to force all these things through. It means I've got to work with other people, I need human help. If I believe in doing music as a way of life, if I want to be a photographer, if I want to run a record company, if I want to write screenplays or poems, whatever I do, whatever I am interested in, go ahead and do that. Be in it with both feet; make a commitment to yourself and to this thing that you love so much, this art, this activity.

"The history of everything that we do, that we think about as the entertainment industry, this business of show and all this, it's all DIY. You know, Thomas Edison was a failure. His little cylinder thing didn't turn out the way he wanted it to. But out of that, he invented the record business. The movie business, even the big studios that today we look at like the enemy, the big record companies, the big corporations—they all started out as DIY. Warner Brothers was a family in Youngstown, Ohio, who had a hardware business. And one of them was a tinkerer and they had this new invention called a movie projector and they got these little reels and put it up in the back of the hardware store and showed these images and charged people and everybody said, 'Oh, this is fantastic!'

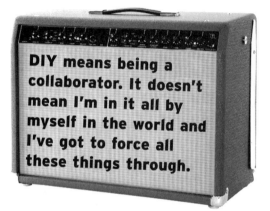

DIY means being a collaborator. It doesn't mean I'm in it all by myself in the world and I've got to force all these things through.

"And so the brothers said, 'This is better than a hardware business. We need more of these films. Where can we get more films?' They didn't have any, so they said, 'Well, let's go make some of these films.' They were following the thing that they were interested in. Their passion was business; they wanted to make a lot of money. So they came to California and started a little business called Warner Brothers.

"Berry Gordy Jr. started Motown Records by borrowing five hundred dollars from his father. Brett Gurewitz started Epitaph Records by borrowing five thousand dollars from his father. Russell Simons started Def Jam with seven hundred dollars. So it's always DIY and that isn't to say that you can't make an accommodation with the gatekeepers, the evil major labels.

"We have to take our pigs to the marketplace, but you can do that in a DIY way by protecting yourself, by learning your job, and taking responsibility for what you are doing.

"Learn how to read a contract; learn what sync rights are; learn what publishing splits are. This is your business. Learn how to file your own taxes; learn how to set up your own health care. Nobody is going to do this for you. If you want to do this for the rest of your life; if you want to do this for your job; if you want to pay your rent doing these kinds of things, the things that you love doing, then you have to take that responsibility.

"When we started Muscle Tone Records, we went to the federal government, to the Small Business Administration, to get a startup loan. They said they had a loan plan for women and minorities, and my wife is Lebanese and really is a woman, so we figured that she should apply. And they didn't make it easy on us. We had to go to business school and had to re-apply three different times to get the loan.

"And one of our professors in business school told us about the concept of practicing sales prevention. That seems to be what the record companies do today. They're suing their own customers (who they allege are stealing music online). It's surreal.

"We're in an exciting time. The whole thing is being shook and shaken and it's all going to come out different and it's always a good time to start your own enterprise, to get together with a couple of your partners and your homeboys and homegirls and say 'let's make something happen. Let's do something.' Because it's the only way that things work."

HOW NOT TO RUIN YOUR MUSIC CAREER

1. You must be the prime mover on any action. No one else will do it.
2. The worse defeat can be the start of your greatest victory.

18
STRAIGHT TALK ON DIY

One of the best things about the DIY Convention is that we bring together people from all facets of the business to discuss specific issues in front of a questioning, probing, and generally cynical audience.

A particularly great panel happened in New York a few years back. We enlisted a collection of people from all points of the record industry spectrum to discuss the indie, major or DIY question.

Moderated by Julie Gordon, a former A&R executive and founder of The Velvet Rope, the record industry's top discussion forum, the panel consisted of Jim Fouratt, a long-time music industry activist who has been involved in the New York club scene, did A&R at a major label, and was a publicist for a time; Bob Chiappardi, the head of Concrete Marketing, which specializes in hard rock music and had a distribution label deal with BMG; Michael Hausman, the manager of Aimee Mann and the head of the United Artists Coalition, which seeks to empower DIY artists; Scott Blasey from the Clarks, which started out as a DIY band, built an enormous following from a regional base, signed with a major and then went back to DIY'ing with the assistance of an indie label; Dave Roberge, the manager of O.A.R., which sold 150,000 copies of its first three albums on their own label before signing with Interscope; and Michael

Caplan, who had a 21-year career at a major label and then left to start his own record and publishing company, OR Music, scoring a tremendous independent success with Los Lonely Boys.

What was interesting about this particular panel was the candor exhibited by the veteran panelists before a packed audience, unusual in an industry that trumpets its successes and buries its failures.

JULIE GORDON: I'm going to start with a basic premise and then open it up to the panelists for conversation. Even in the early '80s, people that were on indie labels were on them hoping to get scooped up by a major label. The goal was, "get on an indie, get attention, and then a major will sign you and you will make it big and you will make lots of money." And a lot of bands spoke about the crooked practices engaged in by some of the indie labels and felt they'd get a better deal on a major label, which had resources the independent labels didn't have.

Now the tables have turned and executives are leaving major labels to start their own thing. Artists whose contracts expire are going out on their own. Just today in one of the local L.A. papers, there's an interview with John Mellencamp, who is now on no label and he says that suits him just fine, because he's already built a base. What he does is go out and tour for three months and then, when he's off the road and he needs another chunk of cash, he'll do another major label deal. But at this point, there's nothing new they can do for him.

MICHAEL CAPLAN: I'll start by saying that the major label model is broken. And before it fell apart and spewed me out as a piece, I decided to quit. I had originally started in Boston working for Morris Levy, who was one of the pioneering independents. I went into a major label 21 years ago and then did A&R for Epic for 17 years. And in that time, I signed bands like Living Colour and G Love and Keb Mo, and Ginuine. There were artists where I would actually get a shot and they got work and they got promoted and everything worked out. There were also always plenty of times where things didn't work out. But what I've seen over the last 21 years is that, increasingly, there is an inability of the majors to get anything to first or second base. I mean, they would put out 100 acts a year and they would work 10, of which two or three would be a hit. I finally got to the stage where the last band I signed made a record for $300,000, because I had the money to make it. Frankly, I could have made the same record for $30,000 if I was pressed to—and then the company spent zero marketing it. They just decided it wasn't one of those worth spending money on. And I was warned early on when I started in A&R, I was told by one of my bosses, 'Don't ever get too close to your artists. Don't let it get personal.' And I couldn't deal that way. I wanted to be close to the creative process and that's why I did A&R. And to have somebody tell me not to care, I couldn't sleep at night. I finally realized that in order to further the artists that I worked with, I would have to get out of that environment, because in the major label model now, all they want to do is hit home runs. They would rather hit 30 home runs a year and strike out 150 times than value anything about getting on first and second base. And there's plenty of world out there to do that kind of stuff. The other thing about the major labels that I find really bad is in the entire time I was an A&R guy, people would always say, 'I'm a song guy. I'm a song guy. I'm a song guy.' And I like great songs. But I'm an artist guy. I mean, I want career-oriented artists. And that was not encouraged at all. The majors now will just break songs. We're teaching people that there's only one good song on a record and, in point of fact, we're only putting one good song on a record. And that's messed up and I refused to deal with that anymore, so I quit. I really think it's the dawning of a new era. And I'm happy to be a part of it.

JULIE GORDON: I think it would be interesting to hear from Scott, because the Clarks were signed to MCA and dropped after one album. Now they're with Razor & Tie and I'd be interested in knowing why you didn't choose to go back to DIY. What are the advantages to a smaller label?

SCOTT BLASEY: The big advantage for us was distribution. We did go back to DIY after we got dropped. We decided to put out a live album to keep up the interest with our fan base. We then started recording the new record and Razor & Tie came on board after we were pretty much done with it. And the main reason for us was distribution. They have it in all the stores and that's helped a great deal.

JULIE GORDON: Michael Hausman. Aimee has been through so much in her career. She was in a group; then did a solo career; then on Epic; there was Imago, Geffen, which then became Interscope; and now she's doing her own thing.

MICHAEL HAUSMAN: That's all of them. But Epic was with the band 'Til Tuesday. Aimee's case is interesting because she was somebody who was on a major label and decided to get off simply because she really didn't enjoy the process, working with the label. She wanted to make records on her own without interference from the A&R people and she wanted to be able to promote the records how she felt they should be promoted. She didn't want to have her arm twisted to do all sorts of crazy promotions that she didn't think were appropriate for her. So we decided to do it on our own. We've been really fortunate and it's worked out really well. She has a very loyal fan base and we've been able to pretty much do everything that I would think a larger label would do. We have a very small label that I run out of my office with just a few people. But I think this is an unusual case because she's well known. I think it's a lot different for somebody who's just starting out.

But whether you're on a major label or on an independent label or you're doing it yourself, I think you do have to have the attitude that you are doing it yourself every day. Because I have an artist right now on a major label and I wouldn't want the project to be anywhere else.

JULIE GORDON: Why?

MICHAEL HAUSMAN: It's actually a trio. I manage Pete Droge, and he just signed a deal with Columbia with Matthew Sweet and Shawn Mullins. We did a trio record and it's not his whole career; it's a project. It's something that I think needs to be on the radio and heavily promoted. And I couldn't think of a better place for it to be, quite honestly. He has his own studio in Washington State and he produces his own solo records. I certainly wouldn't want to bet his whole career on being on a major at this point, but it's good that this project is there.

So, anyway, I've been through many deals with indies and majors. I've had indies do absolutely nothing for my bands. I've had majors do quite a bit for my bands. I've had majors do nothing for my bands. So I don't see any clear rules other than you're always doing it yourself. The only way to approach this business is you have to do everything yourself.

JULIE GORDON: Dave Roberge, you started out totally DIY and built a huge following and the majors came chasing. So how has that been and how is it running the Everfine label?

DAVE ROBERGE: It's an interesting question. I agree with Michael on what he says about DIY. I mean, no matter where you are in your career, whether you start off out of your basement or you're selling three million records on Columbia, you have to be attached to your career because it requires you to be emotionally involved. The first thing I said to O.A.R. when we started working together was to "go home and educate yourselves on this business of music.

And understand all the elements that are out there and how all these elements work together; then come to me and let's answer all the questions we need to before we decide to go out there and start something." And with that particular band, it was the ideal DIY story, because it started with a group of guys who were childhood friends and were playing in the basement and were a high school band and, upon graduating from high school, their friends went off and spread their CDs to all these different college campuses and over the Internet. What we've tried to do is take everything step by step and be patient with it. Never once did we have a goal at the end of the day in mind. It was 'take things as they come to you and make the most of them.' But understand what it is that you're trying to do. For this particular band, it is touring that really is the strength and driving force behind what we do.

Not every band that I talk to or work with is a touring-based model. A lot of bands that I work with might be radio-driven and there are certain labels that might be good to work with. But it's for the artist to really decide first and foremost what route they want to take. If they're not educated and they don't take the time to understand what type of career they want to go after...with my guys, they wanted to be around for 20-30 years. Whether or not that's going to happen, they're going to be the masters of their own destiny in terms of controlling that. For me, it's refreshing, because a lot of artists don't understand what it takes to get from Point A to Point B. They want to go from Point A to Point X, but there are a lot of little steps you need to take before you get there and you have to be very patient. For some, it comes at a faster pace than others. Never compare yourself to anyone else. Don't put yourself onto somebody else's expectations. Set your own goals and work your ass off until you reach them. What we try to do is work really hard to put ourselves in a position to get the music to as many people as possible. I think for any independent label, it comes down to distribution. Distribution, right now, is controlled by the five major companies. At some point, you need to align yourself with a distributor. We've been fortunate enough to be aligned with ADA, which is an AOL Time Warner company (ED: which later was sold). That might scare everybody, but to be honest with you, it's a level of distribution that is necessary because we've been able to strategically micro-market this band, region by region all the way. Two years ago, if we had signed with a major label, that wouldn't have happened, and the words "artist development" would have been lost. For us, it's all about artist development. It's all about taking those steps to get to that next point and building an infrastructure.

MICHAEL CAPLAN: O.A.R. is a really interesting story to look at, because they are a really big live band. But in point of fact, they're not really a jam band, so they've really made it on a total grassroots basis. But what's interesting is you guys were shopping a major label deal perhaps a year ago. And we'd sit in our A&R meetings every week and the subject would be brought up, and then all the tastemakers, who usually comprise A&R, because O.A.R. is just a song-based, traditional kind of band, they would go, "Oh, this sucks! I can't believe it. No way we're going to look at this." Every week we would bring it up and bring it up, and finally someone would go, "Look, they've sold 100,000 records. We should look at this." And then our boss is like, "Forget it!" Because they're not cool. And unfortunately, a lot of what happens at the major label in terms of A&R is, it's got to be very cool and alternative. Unfortunately, O.A.R. doesn't fit that. O.A.R. just makes records that sell. What a wonderful thing!

JULIE GORDON: Well, this is a good segue, because I was just going to address Jim Fouratt and say that Jim spent time working at Mercury Records before the PolyGram/Universal merger. I think that this was a job that had been looked forward to, correct me if I'm wrong, and that it didn't live up to the expectations that you were hoping for. I wanted Jim to address what it's really like at a major label compared to working on a more independent level and what advice you can give to anyone here who feels that they really need to immediately go after that major label deal.

JIM FOURATT: Does anyone here think they have to go after a major label deal? Okay. So that's settled. And thank God! Major labels today are very different from the kinds of places that Michael and I and those of us worked at prior to 1998, when the mergers and acquisitions and downsizing started. Mercury doesn't exist as a label anymore. It has no active staff. When I went to work at Mercury, I went to work for Danny Goldberg, who was a pretty innovative music insider. One of the things he promised me was that I would have my own developing artist label. I could do a little indie label within the context of a major label. And I was given very small budgets—$25,000—imagine trying to sign an artist with a lawyer to a major label for $25,000, but that was the deal—and we signed five acts, we made five records, they were all about to be launched at SXSW in 2000. But the plug got pulled when Mercury and Goldberg went out. And none of those records ever saw the light of day. Now, this is a very sad story. Luckily, those records were so cheap that the artists could have bought them back if they wanted to. But what the disillusionment did to three of those bands is, they broke up. They hated me. They thought it was my fault. And I felt really terrible about that. But it was a lesson well learned. And I want to tell you, no matter how nice the guy or gal might be at the major label who really believes in your band, you have to step back and ask yourself, "Would it be better to have them as a friend? Or to have them as someone that's bringing you into a company?" And I would suggest to you that it would be better to have them as a friend who likes your music. The bands that have been mentioned—Pete Droge, Aimee Mann, The

Clarks—are all stories of artists that really did not succeed at the major label level to the degree that a major label would want them to. They're all artists of merit. Aimee Mann was able to survive all of the tumultuous events that happened professionally to her and still be creative. That is very unusual. Most artists cannot survive being signed and dropped. The Clarks are an example of what can happen. Pete Droge is an artist that was given a lot of backing by a major label and an artist of absolute merit, in my book. I tried to sign him years ago. But he never sold the amount of records that justified the amount of money that was spent on him. And I wonder if he still owes money to that record company. Hopefully not. So get all of that out of your head.

I also will tell you what John Langford said at a panel with me a couple of years ago at SXSW—he was asked, "What's the difference between a major label and an indie label?" And he said, "Nothing. They will both fuck you over." The only thing that's different is the major label has to pay you; the indie doesn't. So be your own label.

John Mellencamp was an artist on Mercury who nobody liked. Not one executive at Mercury under the regime that I was in would say they cared about John Mellencamp. He was not given any attention. He sold 500,000 records instead of a million records or two or three million. He went to Columbia and I think they probably spent some money on him and that was a record that I felt should really have been taken to radio and brought home. They didn't do it. So he's on his own. But John Mellencamp, like many artists today of that ilk, meaning they have that fan base, there's no reason for them to stay on a major label unless that major label make them a number one priority, and they're not. When I worked at Mercury, I signed a band from North Carolina called Craven Melon. It sold 120,000 records in the Carolinas. They repackaged that record, and what did they do? They tried to sell it back to the Carolinas, where it had been No. 1 on radio for 25 weeks and sold 120,000 copies, and then said, "We can't move any product!" Rather than trying to break the band out someplace else, that band was dropped and eventually broke up. That was a band that was grossing a million dollars a year on their own as an independent label. When they signed to a major, they lost money. So it's not about money. Indentured slavery—go see *Biggie & Tupac*. If you haven't seen that film, go see it, because it's really fucking scary. Nobody in this industry would talk out about what the truth was behind the business partnerships that existed around those artists. They were too afraid. That's a very good, extreme example of what can happen to you when you become an indentured slave, as some artist on Mercury once said, rather than becoming your own boss. Be your own boss. You have dignity. You're able to market yourself.

I helped sign a woman named Cindy Bullins to a label and they marketed a very good rock record as a recording by a woman who had lost her baby. Now, who the hell wants to put on a record about somebody's dead baby?!!! Nobody who has a child. She was in a demographic where adults who had young children would know who she was, but no one wanted to play it. But that's how the record company marketed that record. They thought it was an easy way to catch the media and kill the artist. You can maintain control of your own image if you do it yourself and you can wake up at the end of the week and know just how much money you made and where it went or where it didn't go.

JULIE GORDON: I'd like to address Bob Chiappardi, who's the head of Concrete Marketing. I believe, but I could be wrong, that Concrete was formed at a time when hard music was in its heyday, shall we say. I was wondering how the music market has changed what you do at Concrete and if you could speak to your experience with BMG having a label there and why you think that didn't work out so well.

BOB CHIAPPARDI: Well, first, a correction. I started Concrete Marketing 18 years ago with my ex-partner, Walter O'Brien, and it was actually when metal was not in its hey-day. And that's what made it possible to exist. It was a time when the major labels were promoting bands like Haircut 100 and things like that. And they had no real respect for heavy metal. We were kind of a DIY company, in a sense. We were doing things that the record labels didn't. A friend of mine actually described it: "the major labels treat heavy metal like a dirty Kleenex;" which was really what they did. We were like the guys who fix your car or mow your lawn. It was like, sure, we'll give them some money and let them do it; we don't want to deal with it. And the bands that we were working at the time—the first band that I worked was a lit-tle baby band called Metallica. The whole metal thing rose from there. And the bands were working, we grew with them. And once it really started to catch on, the majors said, "Okay." Then they started making their own metal departments and started basically trying to capitalize on the genre exploding.

That's the way the labels work. You have the artists that are out there and they go their own route and they do their own stuff, and one of them catches, and then they start signing up everything in the world that sounds like the one that does really well. Whether it's Guns N' Roses or Pearl Jam or Nirvana...you can name any band out there. But the interesting thing is that most of those bands had to strug-gle to get a record deal because they were different.

I think that a lot of the points that were made here today are about the artist staying true to what they want to do no matter how tough it is. Go your own route and if your music is good and if you're really the kind of artist that has some-thing special, the fans will find you, the word will spread, and the next thing you know, the majors will be kicking down your door, trying to sign you. Again, you have to make a decision. I can't agree 100 percent, but sometimes I think a major label is a good thing to do, if the label deal is done the right way. There are a lot of times when a major can bring you things that you can't do on your own. But the bottom line is you still gotta just stay true to what you feel you're about, because the kids, the fans, they see when it's not real. And you may have a hit song and a hit record today, but tomorrow, you're going to be flipping burgers at McDonald's. Not that it's a bad thing. But you understand what I'm saying.

JIM FOURATT: I forgot two things. One is I never made as much money as I made at Mercury Records and it was nice. But it really corrupts one's integrity if that's what one's doing it for. I make very little money now and my lifestyle hasn't changed from what it was before, except I can't travel as much. The other is, if anyone in this room actually is in a boy band or wants to be a Britney Spears or makes that kind of pop music, I want to say that it's not about the genre of music that you make. Manufactured records are many times pop gems. There is a reason why they get played on the radio and why millions of people buy them. If that is who you are, then perhaps this isn't the room to be in. But don't be ashamed of that. Don't try to be something else. The producers and the re-mixers right now are setting the stage of radio, for the most part. And if you're one of those people, I would suggest you get a very good lawyer, make a very good record, and sell it for many, many dollars. You can dispose of the artists, because that's what happens in those kinds of music projects. The voice is not as important as the choreographer.

JULIE GORDON: I also wanted to add that, in talking at the table before this started, we mentioned that in the new year, probably at least three major labels will cease to exist, possibly even more. That's why this entire DIY thing is so important. Because even if you wanted to be on a major label, as no one here raised their hand that they want to, you can't. It's so hard. What you need to have achieved on

154

D
I
Y

your own right now to get signed to a major label is ridiculous. Artists who were given two and three albums to succeed in their career, sometimes more, wouldn't even have a record deal today, such as Bob Dylan, Bruce Springsteen, a lot of artists. A lot of it has to do with the fact that we got rid of the single. People don't want to pay for a CD, even if they get a lot of bonuses and a DVD with it. They don't want to pay for a CD of 12 songs they don't like just for that one song they do like.

JIM FOURATT: But the new technology is bringing back the concept of a single and it's very hard to get an album listened to. It's all about MP3s and the song. And all of you that are ripping and tearing are probably not ripping and tearing albums, but a song that you like. And I think it's a real challenge to the artist to not just be single-oriented. That's what the technology has become and that is the focus today, about THE SONG, rather than the conceptual album.

JULIE GORDON: I wanted to talk about how the emerging technology has changed things. How has the Internet changed things?

MICHAEL CAPLAN: Well, obviously, there were great expectations a few years ago by a lot of companies that started businesses that were premature. But right now distribution is a little bit confused. The way I'm seeing it is that the MP3 giveaway will replace the single; it'll just be sent out there as a marketing tool. If you need Top 40 radio or alternative radio, which is basically the same thing, then you need a major label, because that's a lot of money. And this addresses what I'm doing at my company. I'm trying not to do singles, but careers. I want career-oriented artists. I don't want songs. And I'm dealing with a 25+ mentality in terms of the consumer I'm going after, because they didn't grow up downloading. They may still download, but it doesn't replace the actual physical manifestation of music. They want to see the liner notes.

JULIE GORDON: Can you tell us some of the artists on your label, just to give people a sense?

MICHAEL CAPLAN: The first artist that I've signed is a girl named Essence, from San Francisco. She was a major label casualty. She made a record for RCA where the A&R guy hired Bill Bottrell, who produced Sheryl Crow. They spent a million dollars. They never finished the record. They shelved it. My second act is a group called Tower of Power, which has been around for 30 years. My favorite band from when I was a kid, and I've been making records with them at Epic for 15 years and they sell 75,000 every time. There's no tour support, there's no marketing money, there's no promotional money, there's no video. And Epic basically let me have them when I left, because they didn't want them. And the third act is this group called Los Lonely Boys that I'm selling through Willie Nelson's production company. Three young Texican brothers from Austin, it's like Stevie Ray Vaughan meets the Everly Brothers. As an indie, I can afford to spend $100,000 making a record and procuring the artist and making you whole. I can spend $150,000 marketing your record. With my model of 25,000 records, both of us are extremely profitable. I don't expect that that's all I want to do. I want to sell millions. But to actually make it so the economy of scale works that we can both help each other. We're both DIYs, in that sense. I can't speak for indie labels that haven't paid their bills in the past, but my company is totally set up and it's a legitimate organization. And the reason I left the majors is that I don't want to rip off people anymore.

JIM FOURATT: But there are some labels that are connected with major labels, like Lost Highway, which has a real clear identity of who they are and the artists that they have.

They've developed Ryan Adams, but they also signed Willie Nelson. Lucinda Williams had hit a plateau on the amount of records she could sell at Mercury, and she sold more records on her last release than she did previously through Lost Highway. So it's really about looking very closely if you want to go that route at who's there, who's in charge and how detached they are, except for distribution and some marketing dollars, from that major label. So it is not that it can't be done, but it's very, very rare that you have a label like Lost Highway.

JULIE GORDON: If you're an indie label and you sign a band, do you have to throw the idea of MTV out the window?

BOB CHIAPPARDI: The answer is yes. You can't do it.

JULIE GORDON: Tell us some things you toss out the window.

MICHAEL HAUSMAN: You toss a lot of things out the window. You can toss out a major radio campaign.

JULIE GORDON: How much does a major radio campaign cost?

MICHAEL HAUSMAN: You can spend as little as $250,000. You can spend as much as a million dollars. But it's a crooked system. You actually pay for play.

MICHAEL CAPLAN: It depends on the radio format, really. If it's Triple AAA, you can spend $50,000, which, although corrupt, not that corrupt. If you're going Modern A/C, it's $150,000. If you're going Top 40, millions. Absolute millions.

MICHAEL HAUSMAN: And that's just one song.

JIM FOURATT: Where are you finding Triple AAA for $50,000? That's almost as expensive as Top 40 in a way, because that's all the middle market.

MICHAEL CAPLAN: Modern A/C, $150,000. Top 40 is like two million to actually get in the door. You've got to have that money in the bank. $50,000 at Triple AAA will buy you a Top 10 record at the format. It's unfortunate that you actually have to pay for play there, but the economy of scale is much smaller. You could pay $1000 for a Level 1 station, $800 for a Level 2, and $500 for a Level 3. Where if you're doing Top 40, forget it. You're doing junkets and houses and boats.

JULIE GORDON: So, then, how does a DIY band get on the radio?

DAVE ROBERGE: I think the best way is to understand radio and respect radio. And I think it starts with a lot of people in this room. It starts with college radio. One of the things that we've tried to do is recognize that, possibly financially, or just out of not wanting to, that we didn't want to put together a radio campaign where we were pushing a particular single. This band, that I've been privileged to work with, is a song-driven band, but not in terms of a single-oriented band. And it goes back to the question of the Internet as well. I don't fear downloading as much as I fear the kids with a CD burner. That's the problem. The downloading of music is going to happen. People are going to go out and try to grab a taste. But if you're an artist that is just writing singles and you're not going to separate yourself and define yourself as an artist—and there's a lot of bands that say, "Oh, I know that band. They do that song." Well, if you fall into that category, you're hurting yourself. I think that the Internet can be a tool as far as an online campaign, as far as our marketing is concerned with this particular artist; we see it as a competitive

D
I
Y

advantage, and we try to embrace all of the new technolo-
gies, try to deliver it.

In terms of radio, it makes it somewhat difficult
because a lot of it comes down to financials. Video also
comes down to financials. These are things that major
labels are obviously able to offer right off the bat, but there
are other things you can accomplish without the use of
radio. You can sell concert tickets; you can sell CDs; you can
sell merchandise; you can do everything that a major label
band can do on your own by understanding those particular steps first and not necessarily relying on radio or a video.
If you're a band that's going to rely on radio and a video,
you're going to have a very short career. But if you're a band
that understands that it starts with your music first and
then the people who are willing to come out and share it
with you and you pay attention to that, then you can build
an infrastructure. But it is a long road and you have to be of
a particular breed.

JIM FOURATT: There's also NPR. NPR is the only national
place that an unknown or regional act can get play and it
will spike sales. A band like Voices on the Verge on Ryko—
they have that little ten-minute section on "All Things
Considered"—those people are not being greased. They listen to the records if you have a way of getting it to them.
And the way of getting it to them is sometimes through
your local NPR outlets and through the critics. That's the
only radio that I know of that will serve the non-major label
artist of quality and merit.

MICHAEL HAUSMAN: And that's national radio that
Jim's talking about. One of the things that I wanted to say
when Dave was speaking is that it's really important to start
locally. Don't worry about a station all the way across the
country that wants to play your record and charge you
$1500 to spin it. Forget about it. You have to start locally. It's
going to be a station in your area where you gig that's going

**D
I
Y**

to play your record and you're not going to have to pay them and if that's not happening, if no one's playing your record locally, it's probably not going to happen anywhere else. So you should just make another record or don't worry about radio. Don't expect things to happen nationally for you before they happen regionally. The same thing goes as far as getting gigs and getting press. There are a lot of people asking, "We're on an indie label and they won't pay tour support." And I'm like, "Well, where do you want to go? Who's going to go see you if you travel 3000 miles to play a show? Don't bother." Play around the corner. Play 20 miles away or 50 miles away. Just play in a radius where you can drive home at night. I really think you have to be very reasonable about your expectations when you start off, especially if you're doing it yourself.

I wanted to just touch on one other thing. Whether you're dealing with a major label or independent label, the real question is ownership. Who owns the recording and who owns the song. When you sign a deal, a traditional deal, what happens is—and this is with an indie or a major—they take everything. "It's ours. You work for us now." If you have a good lawyer, you manage to chisel back some things. You can't release it as a budget record before a certain amount of time passes by; you can't stick it in a TV commercial without asking our permission. There are all these marketing restrictions that you manage to muscle out of them. Forget that. You should own it yourself. You should make it yourself. You should borrow money from your cousin or your dad or whomever you can afford to hit up for money. Or just pay for it yourself. Once you own it, then you can license it.

And licensing is the most beautiful thing ever. I mean, I love the major labels, because when they call me for an Aimee Mann track for a soundtrack album or for a television show or a movie, I know they have really deep pockets and I charge them an insane amount of money. We license it to them. We say, "Here it is. Take it. Take it for your TV show or take it for your soundtrack album." That's really the key: if you own it, you control it. And you only divvy out the rights that you have to divvy out. You want to have it in the stores? Well, you do a deal with a label or maybe it's a Razor & Tie and you say, "Have the record for five years. You can sell it in North America. You can put it in the stores. And that's it. After five years, it comes back to us." There are lots of ways of doing licensing deals. The only way you're really going to control it, is if you own it. Just don't let anybody else own it unless the paycheck is so huge that you're willing to let them screw with it. And that's really where the danger comes in. Because if you take the big money, then they will own it and they'll do whatever they want with it. And you have to be willing to deal with those consequences. I really believe in licensing. And if you talk to your lawyer, say, "I don't want a record deal. I want a licensing deal." It's as simple as that. And this is no new form; it's been going on for years. Licensing is very straightforward. It's a shorter contract. It won't cost you a fortune and you'll own your music.

JIM FOURATT: And you'll only get to that stage where they want to license you when you have done all the other work in a region or locally, where people who know about you want to hear your music.

I also want to talk about the coolness of an indie label and tell you to beware. Knitting Factory Records—very cool among certain kinds of musicians. They'll give you $2000 to make a record. They own the publishing one hundred percent. They own the record. They'll give you no money for marketing. They do no tour support or very tiny tour support. Now, why would they do that? Well, you might want to go there because you think they're going to give you $2000. And they will build a catalog, and Knitting Factory Records now has a catalog of over 400 records. When major labels want to build their catalog they buy these catalogs from the owner of the independent label. You will not participate in that, or you will participate at the lowest level. So do it yourself until, like the Clarks, they come knocking at your door and then still do it yourself. Remember, Dave Matthews had not one single on any of those records that sold close to half a million records. It was only when he went to RCA that they crafted a radio song, because they could not get this act that was selling a huge amount of records on the radio because there were no songs. If you're a band where the song itself is not the most important thing, forget about it. Live where people want and support you. You have to know who you are, what your goal is, and what you won't give up to get something.

JULIE GORDON: I did have one more question to ask Scott from The Clarks. And that would be: what do you think you learned from your MCA experience that you can counsel people here on?

SCOTT BLASEY: I think the biggest thing is you have to experience it. You can sit here and listen to us tell you not to do something. But if somebody waves a big check in front of you and says "let's sign this deal and we're going to make you big," it's really hard not to do that. And we did it, and it didn't work. And I think that process weeds out a lot of musicians. We decided to keep going. We signed an indie deal. And getting back real quick to the ownership of your property, I would say that that's the biggest thing, that we continue to own our independent records and continue to make money off of them, and we still own all of our publishing. So regardless of our label situation, we're still able to play and make money and sell records that can support the band.

HOW NOT TO RUIN YOUR MUSIC CAREER

1. Understand that there are several paths to success.

2. Failure only weeds out the uncommitted.

3. It's not the gross, it's the net.

19
END GAME

The funny thing about the DIY movement in music is that it always gets confused with the punk music underground. Understandable, since they were the very first to use the initials DIY to describe making music outside the system.

But the true DIY movement isn't the province of any one particular genre or movement. It's not even about one set way of doing things. The DIY way is truly about finding what's best for you, about not surrendering any rights that you don't have to surrender, about finding a way to stay in the game and enjoy a long career making music or helping those who do.

The DIY movement of today is actually the music industry of today, not separate camps neatly divided. The so-called "major" record labels are beginning to become boutique outlets, concentrating on a handful of superstars and working them across multiple platforms and releases. It's what major entertainment companies were ultimately designed to do: create worldwide superstars that transcend the day-to-day business of merely making music.

Soon enough, a major record label will have rosters that encompass perhaps 10 artists at any one time. They will work hard to sustain the careers of these artists, crossing them over to the other entertainment areas of the company, making them movie stars, video game stars, merchandise movers, and, oh yes, they also have a recording to sell.

That situation will leave the other 95 percent of the music world to fill the remaining 180 slots on the Billboard 200 Pop Album Chart. And while the overall sales of these artists may not reach the levels that acts once sold in a world where video games and the Internet didn't compete for attention, they will thrive and find their way at lower sales levels, thanks to smarter business practices.

The DIY way is truly about finding what's best for you, about not surrendering any rights that you don't have to surrender, about finding a way to stay in the game and enjoy a long career making music or helping those who do.

Everyone can see the writing on the wall, even people who were once a part of the major label system.

Al Teller was once the chairman of the MCA Music Entertainment Group, which, when he ran it, was one of the six biggest distributors in the world. A few years after leaving MCA, Teller ran one of the first online record labels.

"In the good old days, you really had to go to a record company to get funded," said Teller. "Now, with the kind of technology that's available, it's fairly inexpensive for a young band to take those first tentative steps. They make their own record, they get their own CDs pressed, and they try to sell it locally. You see a lot of that happening. A lot of independent labels have formed to service that contingent. And we've seen the market share of independent labels grow dramatically over the last few years reflecting these trends."

While Teller's foray into the Internet didn't work out—the company arrived way before high-speed connections made downloading music more than sheer agony—he did recognize that the world was gradually changing.

"The major labels really are operating under a sort of paradigm that's been in place for as long as I've been in the business, for 25 years or longer," he said. "And it's just become an unwieldy one. It just doesn't work. The radio marketplace is completely fragmented. The whole notion of marketing really is very different than it used to be in the sense that setup is incredibly, incredibly important; micro-marketing—just following a record around from city to city, using SoundScan (the compiler of chart sales) information to really target your marketing dollars in a straightforward and effective fashion—all of these things come into play. It's very difficult for large, monolithic label structures to handle that for a large number of releases."

That is why the DIY movement as presently constituted will ultimately become the way most record industry business is done. Not only is it smart business practice in action, but DIY also represents virtually the only way that music companies can exist. The enormous competition for attention spans in today's entertainment world means that buying a CD is an increasingly small part of the overall consumer budget.

Keeping control of your master recordings and publishing will allow you the flexibility to control your own destiny as you navigate through this complex world of choices.

Unlike the old timers, you now understand that the choice isn't between nothing or having it done for you. The new watchword for industry success is do it yourself.

And not, as the industry was once constructed, having it done to you.